JEANET'

RANSOMED HEARTS

RANSOMED HEARTS, PART TWO

This is a work of fiction. Names, characters, places, and incidents either are the product of the author's imagination or are used fictitiously.
Any resemblance to actual persons, living or dead, events, or locales is entirely coincidental.

Published by Bardale Press

www.bloginbasket.com

Cover by Jon Stubbington
www.bookcoversbyjon.com

First paperback edition 2022

Ransomed Hearts: the story so far.

In the early 1960s two outsiders fled to Bardale, a village in north Lancashire. They were werewolves, and twins, and their names were Anthony and Tomas. They went by the surname Preston.

They married local girls, Frances and Miriam, and each had a son, Mark and John.

At the end of the decade, when the children were still young, the Preston twins became aware that the threat that they'd run from was moving closer, and they left their families to draw the threat away from Bardale and fight it head on. They travelled to France and did not return.

They had to assume that Bardale was no longer safe for their families, and asked them to move away. Miriam and Frances left their homes and families in Bardale, and took their sons to Ulverston, a large town near the Lancashire coast. They cut all ties with Bardale and began new lives as single mothers in a new place.

We pick up their story nine years later.

Chapter 1

Standing by the graveyard wall, young and vulnerable, hugged up against the cold and the rain, Joyce watched warily as the car drew up. The man who leaned out of the window was in his twenties.

'Are you OK, love?' he asked cautiously.

'I'm fine, are you OK?' she replied. Her voice was neutral.

'Shouldn't you be at home with your parents? A girl your age?'

'I'm seventeen, I can do whatever I want. Or whatever you want,' she replied.

'Do you want me to take you home?' he offered, half convinced that his intention was chivalrous.

She shrugged, and the light from a passing car highlighted the rain on her pale face, the drops gathering at the ends of her soaked long black hair, falling gently to her sodden clothes. She looked so helpless. Then she raised her eyes, and smiled a small, knowing smile.

'Where do you *want* to take me?' she asked.

This time he swallowed. She was fourteen, at the very most, and making no effort to disguise it.

'How much?' he whispered.

'Fifty,' she told him.

He nodded and opened the car door.

Half an hour later, the transaction complete, the girl climbed the graveyard wall and walked for a while between the gravestones. She stopped by a crypt and looked around. She stood stock-still, silent as the stones, listening for breathing, a damp footstep. Eventually, satisfied, she stripped and hid her clothes and the night's wages before starting to shudder convulsively.

Within a minute, a black wolf stood in her place. She sniffed warily at the place she had buried her property, and stalked stiff-legged away from the crypt. She nosed for a while at the freshest graves, then ran, faster and faster, heading for the next wall, not too low, not too high. With a joyous, free leap into space, she cleared the barrier and landed, crouched and alert, in suburbia.

A quick glance and a pause to listen, then she moved to the shadows and made her way through the leafy estate towards home. As she got to her street, she noticed light coming from a bedroom window. She paused to sniff around the front door, her hackles rising, a low growl beginning that she quickly suppressed. She crossed to the other side of the street, concentrating on the open first-floor window, the tiny space offered to her, so high a jump, so routine a challenge.

She gathered herself up and ran, making a sure, swift movement, twisting on her way through to avoid the cling of curtains. *He* was there, soft red-brown hair falling across his face as he bent over her young sister's bed, his hand under the covers.

She leaped.

Chapter 2

The boy prowled the cold streets of the Lancashire town. He'd crept down the stairs of the terraced house, avoiding the creaky step, and let himself out. His mother was asleep, the sleep of the exhausted.

Something made him restless, some tidal pull. He pushed his long dark hair away from his face and looked around. The cold air felt good on his skin, and he stopped for a moment, catching the scent of the sea, only a mile or so away. He knew the local tides and currents like a lover, and he turned seawards.

The incoming tide tempted him to strip off his clothes, and kneel in the surf, letting the chill water caress him, love him. He gauged the currents and the power of the sea against his strength and skill, and stood, ready to wade into the cold depths and strike out for the headland to his right. A stray plastic bag wrapped around his legs and he stumbled, falling face forwards into the water. The surf crashed over his head, and he opened his eyes to a swirl of green and grit that blinded him. He was used to the sea, but for a moment he panicked. He pushed himself up again, suddenly finding himself out of his depth, swept out to sea. He swam, catching the familiar current. As he recovered, he felt a sickening pain in the small of his back … a lump of driftwood had caught him. He was swept forwards again. The sea had lost her allure and he was beginning to get angry. He headed for the beach. A few yards inland from the breaking surf, he stopped and looked for his clothes. The tide had come in faster than he had bargained for, and they were gone. He was cold, wet, naked and annoyed. The feeling of incompleteness was there again, the sense that there was something on the tip of his tongue, something that needed to be expressed. Frustrated, he decided to run home. As he moved over the beach, feet familiar with every contour and rocky outcrop, he felt an overwhelming relief sweep through his body; he felt warmer, stronger, faster, all four paws moving in synchrony.

The young wolf stopped suddenly, a look of surprise in his yellow eyes. He sat on the sea wall licking his fur, examining his feet and twisting around to stare at his long black glossy tail. He bit the tail experimentally and jumped at the pain. It started to wag, and he watched it for a while, before carefully jumping down and making his way through the narrow streets back to his home. Every few minutes he looked at his feet, tripped up, and had to sit for a while before starting to move again. When he reached his front door he sat, perplexed, before making his way to the back of the house. As usual, the kitchen window was open wide enough for a skinny boy to wriggle through, but the thought of trying to jump up in this new and weird body was daunting.

This would take some thought. Mark struggled to remember exactly what had happened on the beach. He followed the stages in his mind and concentrated. After a few seconds of intense agony, he found himself human, vulnerable and naked, lying on the clean swept flags of the back garden path. He dragged himself through the window, and to his bed. He lay awake, thinking hard, making connections and making plans.

Chapter 3

The boys clattered out through the front door, and Miriam sighed. 'His fifteenth birthday. I wish we could have done more.' Frannie reached across the table and squeezed her hand. 'He's had a birthday tea with us and Mark, he's got those records he wanted, and he's off to the cinema. He's fine.'

Miriam managed a smile. 'I'm glad they're so close, it would have been harder, otherwise. And you … you've been a better friend than I ever deserved.'

'Me and thee against the world, eh?' Frannie sat back and sighed. 'How are you today?'

'You know, it comes and goes.' Miriam smiled brightly. There was an edge to it and Frannie understood that today wasn't a good day. 'You'll take care of him, won't you? When it's time?'

'As if he was my own,' Frannie promised. She spoke briskly. 'Is everything sorted? Your will? The house?'

'Just ring the council when it's time. The furniture is mine, free and clear, take what you need and sell the rest, same goes for everything else. I wish I'd been able to hang on to my own house, but…'

'I know, it's hard for a woman on her own.' Frannie had made a decent living over the years, keeping the books for local shops and businesses, but she knew that Miriam had struggled to manage with a string of part-time and temporary jobs. Miriam had always found it easy to get hired, but harder to get a decent wage, and it had only taken a couple of years for her to give up on the mortgage payments for the house she'd bought when they first arrived in Ulverston. She lived in a council house, not far from the terraced house that Frannie had bought.

'It's in my room, on top of the wardrobe. The will.' Miriam winced. 'Along with John's birth certificate. There's nothing else, you know? I made a clean break.'

'I know, love.'

'Any news?' Miriam smiled weakly. It was a joke now, the women understood that there wasn't going to be any news from their husbands. The twins were long gone, and there had been no word from either of them since the day they left.

'No news.' Frannie said. She bit her lip. 'Any message, just in case?'
Miriam looked down and shook her head. 'What would I say? I didn't wait for him, I had boyfriends, he'll understand that. I did my best for John. I just wish I could see John married, settled.'

Frannie laughed. 'You want to live forever?' she joked, and Miriam smiled back.

'No, not forever, but a bit longer would have been nice. We could have had a nice party, for my fortieth. Don at the club would have let me have the function room cheap, the boys could have played their music, you know, like their dads did. Remember? Do you remember?'

Frannie stood up and went to hug her friend, very gently. 'I remember, every minute. We were an odd couple, me and thee, weren't we? The May Queen and the farm girl.'

'The prettiest, cleverest girls in Bardale, my dear.' Miriam giggled. 'My god, the skirts you used to wear. Did you take them off the scarecrows?'

'Hey, they were my mother's. It's not my fault she was three sizes bigger than me! Dad had enough on his plate without me mithering for new clothes, and nobody ever got round to teaching me how to take clothes in.' Frannie heard the defensive tone in her voice and took a deep breath. 'Sorry, still a sore point! You were always so fashionable, even after you got married.'

'Ah well, you found your own style, and it suits you.' Miriam smiled fondly at her friend, who was dressed soberly in a deep crimson blouse with a grey skirt and waistcoat. 'Red was always your colour. Speaking of, before I forget, there are Christmas presents under the bed, for you and Mark and John. I bought them last month, just in case. And I suppose I was right. I hope I didn't jinx it. I mean, I wanted another Christmas, but it's not going to happen.'

'How bad?'

'I've lost five pounds this week. I'm on that many painkillers during the day when John's at school. Weekends are hard, I try to stay off them when he's around, but it's difficult. Who would have guessed that my great life skill would turn out to be juggling painkillers and uppers? Don't answer that, by the way. I reckon this is the conversation, isn't it? Where we sort everything out, before it's too late.'

Frannie's eyes filled with tears and Miriam looked shocked. 'Hey, Frannie, I'm the one who cries. You're the brave one.'

'You've been a sister to me, we only have each other.' Frannie said, choking up with tears.

'Well, you have John and Mark, and they're good lads, so stop feeling sorry for yourself. Now. What do I need to tell you? Oh yes, the will is on top of the wardrobe, the Christmas presents are under the bed, and I want to be buried in that pink dress that I've had since forever. It'll fit me again now. I always knew that I'd diet back into it one day. Full make-up, just in case the boys want to see me afterwards. If they don't, that's OK, don't force it. And don't send word to Bardale. We've been safe so far, so let's not spoil things, eh?' She reached for her handbag and took out a scrap of paper. 'These hymns, at the funeral. Nothing miserable, have a good old singalong and think of me. I've talked to the vicar and he's promised to go easy on the God stuff and aim things towards the boys, remembering the good times. Nice bloke, better than that miserable Kendrick chap who did old Mrs Forsyth's funeral.' She fell quiet. 'Cuppa?'

'I'll make it,' Frannie said; the kitchen was as familiar as her own.

'Just water for me. Tea makes me nauseous,' Miriam whispered.

Frannie came back from the kitchen with a long glass of water and a mug of tea. Miriam's eyes were closed. Frannie sighed. 'You're exhausted, shall I go?'

'No, I want to wait up for John, see his birthday out. You know? Stay here with me, Mark can walk home with you when they get back.'

They sat in silence for a while, and then Miriam stood and put a record on the turntable. 'Everlys,' she said. 'For old times' sake.'

They listened to both sides of the record, smiling but not speaking. Miriam stood and carefully put the vinyl away. 'If Tomas does come back, give him this record. Tell him I never stopped thinking about him.' She closed her eyes. 'I'm going to have a little nap. Wake me up when the boys are home.'

Chapter 4

The back door clicked shut and Frannie stood up. She knew every noise in the house, and that particular click meant that Mark was home. She closed the ledger that she was working on and went downstairs. Mark was filling the kettle. 'Coffee?' he asked. 'Thank you, love.'

'You're working?' Mark frowned.

Frannie nodded. 'I usually work on Saturdays, maybe I'll try to keep the day clear now that you're home.'

'Oh, it's OK. I mean, I'll find something to do.'

Frannie sat down at the kitchen table and looked at her son. He looked lost. Saturdays had always been spent at Miriam's. Now Miriam was gone, and John was tackling the first day of his new Saturday job at the local market. Mark didn't know what to do with the day, and he was just realising that his mother had a whole routine that didn't include him.

'Do you have homework?' Frannie asked.

'Did some last night, we usually do it together. We'll finish it tonight' Mark lit the gas hob and put the kettle on. He took three mugs from the cupboard then shook his head and put one back. 'Can I get a Saturday job too?'

'Yes, in March, when you're fifteen. Where've you been?'

'Walked to the market with John, then walked back.' He blinked. 'Can we go to the beach?

We used to go with Miriam sometimes.'

'Well, it's getting a bit cold for that.' Frannie registered Mark's lost look and sighed. 'OK, let's have this drink, then I'll put the books away and we'll go. I can spare a few hours.'

The beach was pebbled and cold, but it had an ice cream van and a wall where Frannie and Mark could sit and watch the waves lap at the stones. Frannie shivered inside her anorak and waited. She knew her son, and knew when a storm was brewing.

'I thought there'd be someone at the chapel, you know?' he said eventually.

'Someone?'

'Someone from Auntie Miriam's family. But it was just us, and the vicar, and the people from her work, and a couple of her old boyfriends.'

'Ah,' Frannie whispered.

'I'm old enough to know,' Mark said, his voice carefully controlled.

'Yes, you are. But I can't tell you, however old you are. We've been over this.'

'Why not? Where's my dad? My grandparents? Do I have any aunties or uncles? Cousins? Where did you and Miriam come from?'

'I can't tell you.' Frannie said levelly. 'One day, I might be able to, but I don't know when that day will be. And I know it's hard on you, and I'm sorry, but it doesn't change things.'

'How can you do this to me?' Mark asked. He stood up, gathered a handful of stones and started throwing them into the sea. Frannie winced.

She knew every line of him; he was the mirror of her, and she recognised his righteous hurt. She stayed silent and waited for the tears. When Mark turned back to her, he was dry-eyed. He glared at her. 'I'll find out, one day.'

'Maybe, but I'm doing my very best to stop you doing that. It's for your own good, and mine too, so if you could wait a few more years I'd be very grateful.' She managed a smile. He stared at her; this was more information than he'd ever been given before.

He licked his lips and moved closer. He lowered his voice. 'Is there anything about the family, about you, or my dad, or John's dad that's … different? Anything I should know?'

Frannie stared at him. 'Whatever do you mean? No. Why would you ask something like that?'

'Nothing, nothing Mum. Forget it.' He swallowed hard. 'I miss her. She was more than an auntie, you know?'

'I know. I can't take her place. We talked about you boys all the time, and she told me not to try to be her, because it would just be embarrassing.' Frannie shook her head. 'Imagine, me trying to be Miriam.'

'Don't try.' Mark was struggling not to smile. 'She could never be you, and you could never be her.' He stared out to sea. 'Do you think John's dad will come back for him, now that Miriam's dead.'

'No.' Frannie said. 'Can we close that subject? You know I won't talk about it.'

She watched as the anger blossomed briefly

in Mark's eyes, then faded. He nodded. 'Sure. No point in fighting, eh? It's me and you against the world and we shouldn't fight.'

'Me and you and John.' Frannie sighed. 'Come on, let's go home, I'm freezing.'

Back at home, they had a brief, silent lunch, then went to the garden shed, where they fitted two hooks into a wooden beam, setting them eighteen inches apart. 'To dry your shoes, after the market.' Frannie smiled. 'I have enough customers working there to know that they're not allowed in the house with their work shoes on.'

John arrived home, quieter than usual. He actually looked tired, which was unusual enough for Mark to remark on. John put a cloth shopping bag next to the sink and turned to Frannie. 'I asked for some of my pay in kind, like you said. They gave me a rabbit and half a dozen eggs. Is that OK?' He dug into his pocket and pulled out three crumpled pound notes. 'Just three quid this week, because it was training, and I didn't do much, but he says six after that, and if I want to do some Thursdays during the holidays I can. Oh, and Mr Hubbard from the fish stall said he would give me his books next week to bring to you, save him a trip, and he asked me when Mark turns fifteen because he needs a Saturday boy next year. Here…' He pushed the money towards Fran, proud of himself. ' for my keep.'

She pushed it back. 'It's yours; this is your home, you don't pay for your keep, but thanks for the food – it all helps. We'll have a nice rabbit stew on Monday, eh?' She turned away and left the room. John looked so much like Tomas and Anthony, and he'd done exactly the same thing that Anthony used to: passing his wages over to be divided up for bills and food and clothes and fun. It had been a while since there'd been any fun.

After tea, she brought a box down from the attic and took out a dozen old LPs. Miriam's record player was now in the living room, along with her records. She turned the TV off and switched the record player on. 'Boys, come and listen,' she called. The boys joked about the old records, but after a while John started to sing along. Frannie hadn't heard him sing for years; he'd got self-conscious while his voice was changing, but it sounded like it had pretty much settled now.

That night, Frannie woke briefly when she heard a noise. Two boys talking, trying to be quiet, in the middle of the night. They didn't sleep much, those two. Like their dads. She sighed and closed her eyes; she had a job to do, keeping them safe, and she knew it wasn't going to be easy. Tomorrow she'd persuade John to accompany her and Mark to chapel. Miriam hadn't been a churchgoer, but Frannie wasn't going to leave John in the house alone. The boy had a fine voice on him, and a place in the choir would be a distraction. She had a feeling she'd need to keep John very busy over the next few years.

Chapter 5

Mark pressed his back against the wall of the sixth form college library and watched half familiar faces come and go. It was, he reflected, a stupid place to arrange to meet his cousin; one of the cafes would have been more sensible.

He was about to give up and leave when he glimpsed John out of the corner of his eye. That hair was unmistakable; nobody else had so much of it, long piratical black curls framing angelic features and innocent dark eyes. The owner of those deceptive eyes was holding hands with a pretty blonde. Mark glanced at the Lady Di hairdo, the punky blue-and-pink eye make-up, the embroidered denim jacket and the New Romantic blouse. No commitment, he thought, and dismissed the girl from his attention.

'You're late,' he observed.

'Got chatting to Elaine. She was at Parkside as well; funny how we never knew her there, isn't it? Anyway, she's doing geography too, she was enrolling in front of me.'

'Excellent. You're still late.' Mark grumped.

Elaine looked from one boy to the other and excused herself. She cast one last look back at them and was rewarded with a cheery wave from John.

'Are you sure you didn't go out with her last Easter?' Mark asked.

'That was Aylene.' John said, already looking round, scoping out the room. 'It's a big library, loads of nooks and crannies for snogging in.'

'They're called reading booths,' Mark said, a smile reluctantly surfacing. John was impossible, and he knew it. 'Anyway, come on, I need some fresh air and it stopped raining ten minutes ago.'

The cousins walked outside, finding an unoccupied bench. Mark wiped away the last of the rain with his handkerchief, and they sat down, happy to people-watch.

'All sorted now?' John asked.

'Uh-huh. Music, maths, English language, general studies.' Mark took out a timetable and frowned at it. 'I've not got many free periods either. What did you sign up for?'

'Music, geography, Spanish, general studies.'

'Spanish?' Mark raised an eyebrow. 'You've never done Spanish before.'

'Yeah, I reckon I'll fail miserably, drop it later, get more free time.' John said casually. Mark got the feeling that this education business was not John's priority.

They watched their new fellow students pass by; some of them nodded, recognising the cousins from school. Some of the girls slowed down as they approached, walking straighter as they passed and tossing their hair back casually, raising their voices as they chatted to their friends. Mark kept a cynical smile off his face; none of that was for his benefit. John didn't notice, as it was nothing unusual for him. A group of three walked past, a skinny guy flanked by a sporty-looking girl and an equally athletic-looking guy. All three of them had long fair hair, the athlete's curled almost as extravagantly as John's. They were all dressed in pale blue ripped and patched jeans, and tour T-shirts. Mark cast a jealous eye at the T-shirts, utterly sure that they'd been bought at gigs, not record shops. As he tore his glance away, the thin boy looked his way with naked curiosity. Mark broke the eye contact, looking down, trying not to blush. John noticed. 'He fancies you,' he teased.

'Fuck off,' Mark muttered, but looked up again, watching the trio walk away. He shook his head and stood up. 'Come on, mate, let's go home, we're finished here for the day.'

'Who were they?' John asked, still watching the retreating backs.

'Dunno, bunch of freaks…' Mark said dismissively.

'I feel a great disturbance in the Force,' John said, deadpan. Mark hit his arm affectionately, and they turned for home.

'We have a small class this year, just fifteen of us,' the music teacher said. 'Let's go round and introduce ourselves. You, tall girl, you start.'

The blonde smoothed her hair back and stood up. 'I'm Helen Townsend, from the Willows school, I'm here to study music, maths, biology and chemistry. I'm seventeen and I want to go to university to study science when I finish my A levels.'

John nudged Mark and hissed 'I love older women.' Mark ignored him.

The tutor went round the class, and Mark half listened, watching the blondes in front of him. The three of them were sat together on the front row, a suspicious act in itself. John had dragged Mark to take the back-row seats, and they slouched down together, united against the world, as always. The big athletic bloke was talking. 'I'm Andy Ransome, I was at the Willows too. I'm studying music, English literature, French and history.'

'Get him.' John snorted. 'He's going to Oxford.'

'At least it's a plan,' Mark shot back, unamused, and John subsided, finding a loose screw in the table and rummaging in his bag for something to fix it with.

The teacher smiled. 'You, at the back, the thin boy with the … with the long black hair. Who are you?'

Mark glared at her; he was sure she'd been about to mention his nose. He was getting self-conscious about it; it seemed to get longer and thinner every day. He started to speak, and the teacher … no, the lecturer – he was a real student now, at sixth form college – spoke up. 'No, lad, stand up please, so that we can see you.'

He blushed. The three at the front had turned round, and the skinny blond was grinning at him. He scowled back. 'I'm Mark Preston, I was at Parkside school, and I'm here to study music.'

'What else?' the lecturer prompted him.

He glared, at bay. 'It doesn't matter what else,' he growled. A slow handclap from the front started – it was that skinny blond again, Mark shot him his best dirty look and the lad shrugged and stopped. The girl looked almost sympathetic, and Mark bit his lip; he didn't want sympathy.

The teacher nodded. 'I hope you can live up to that statement,' she said simply. 'Now, you at the back with the dark curly hair.'

John stood up. 'Hiya, I'm John Preston … we're cousins, not brothers.'

'Or married,' the skinny blond interrupted, and the class collapsed in giggles. John stood perfectly still and stared at the blond until he turned round. John continued. 'I'm sixteen, and I was at Parkside. I'm here to study music too, and some other stuff because I have to.'

Finally, the teacher's attention moved back to the front row, to the thin blond who Mark was already suspicious of. 'Hi Xan. I know you, of course, but other people might not.'

'Xan' stood up. 'Hey, I'm Alexander Kendrick, but everyone calls me Xan. I was at the Willows school too. Miss Davison knows me because she was my Sunday School teacher.' He grinned, unashamed. 'I'm here to study music, maths, further maths, physics and social sciences.'

The teacher laughed. 'Xan, we don't teach social sciences here.'

'It doesn't mean I can't study them though,' Xan shot back, and the class relaxed, some of them amused, some already convinced that the guy was a dickhead.

By the end of the class, Mark was beginning

to relax; he'd got the vibe that the lecturer knew that her job was to get them through the curriculum and the exams, but that she was more than willing to make it interesting. She'd already passed round information about low-cost instrument rental and places to practise. He'd listened carefully to the others in the class, and knew that Helen's interest in music was mathematical, but that she could play passable guitar for a girl, and she loved to sing. Ransome was a guitarist and scorned other instruments. That made sense as he looked like a rocker and probably had ambitions to be the next David Coverdale. Kendrick claimed to be a 'percussionist' rather than a drummer, which had drawn a long, slow, sardonic smile from John. The rest of the class included more would-be rock stars and a fair few electro kids who wanted to play synths.

Chapter 6

The days passed, but sixth form was harder than school. It was a big jump from O level standards to A levels, and Mark was struggling a little with the syllabus. His daytime leisure time seemed to have dropped to zero, as when he wasn't at college he was doing homework or preparation, or at work at the fish market on Saturdays, getting smelly and cold but earning a bit of pocket money. John worked there too, at a stall at the opposite end of the market.

One morning he'd just served a customer when his boss nudged him. 'Young lady to see you,' he said. 'Don't be too long.'

Mark looked round, startled, then nodded politely when he saw Helen Townsend standing in the middle of the market, scrupulously far from the wet counters. The crowd of customers unconsciously gave her space, parting around her as she stood looking at him. He hastily washed his hands and walked across to her.

'Hey, has your mum sent you for the shopping?' he asked, cursing himself straight away.

She looked at him coolly. 'We have our fish delivered,' she said quietly. 'I'm actually here to invite you and John to a party at mine, tonight.'

'Tonight?'

'Is that a problem? I've written out the address.'

Mark took the proffered sheet of paper; the address was way out of town, and a long way from a bus stop. He shrugged. 'I'll see, but I can't promise,' he said. 'Who else will be there?'

'The maths crowd, and the music crowd. I thought it would be fun to let them mix.' She smiled and Mark relaxed, feeling included for once. Xan, Helen and Mark were the only students studying both subjects, and had taken to walking together between lessons. It had been Xan's idea to encourage Mark to stick with them, and Mark enjoyed their company. He tucked the address into his back pocket. 'We'll try to make it,' he promised. Helen beamed at him. 'Wonderful!' she said, then made her way out of the wide doors of the indoor market and slid into the front passenger seat of a waiting car. It was long, low and expensive, and the driver was at least thirty. Mark blinked; it was none of his business. He hadn't quite worked out the relationship yet between Helen, Kendrick and Ransome, but it didn't really surprise him to see the self-assured blonde in the company of an older man.

Lunchtime came, and he made his way to the other end of the market. John was at the back of his stall, and Mark found him jointing a rabbit for a customer. Mark delivered the message, and John raised his eyebrows. 'Tonight? Where?'

Mark told him, and John nodded. 'We'll get there, somehow. Is it a birthday?'

Mark shrugged. 'I didn't ask.'

'OK, we'll take some beer. I'll buy it, you'll never get served.' At nearly seventeen, John found it easy to pass as adult. Mark didn't.

On the bus back home they found

themselves with plenty of space, as the other passengers gave them a wide berth. Once back home they put their stinking work shoes on the hooks in the tiny shed, stripped off in the kitchen and loaded their market clothes into the washing machine, setting it on a hot wash. Mark's mum would take it from there. They took turns showering and washing their hair, going through three cycles instead of the usual Saturday night two. When they got downstairs again, Mark's Mum pronounced them 'sweet and clean' and dished out the kedgeree that she'd made for supper.

During the evening meal, Mark carefully broached the subject of the party, and his Mum looked alarmed until Mark showed her the address. She approved. 'They're a good family, the Townsends. Not many of them left, but they're related to the Reverend Kendrick, and to the Ransomes.'

The boys looked at each other. 'The *Reverend* Kendrick?' John said, after eventually swallowing his kedgeree.

'Yes, he's a lovely man, very upright. He's had a terrible life, you know?' Frannie Preston loved to share her knowledge with her son and nephew; she thought that gossip was a sin, but it wasn't the same thing if you were educating the boys in your care, was it?

Mark smiled. 'Why, what happened?'

'Oh, his mother and father were missionaries, and Arthur Kendrick was brought up by his aunts and uncles. He was called to the ministry himself very young, and was working in London among … well, let's say among girls who weren't as good as they should have been. One of those girls was from a good family, and Arthur rescued her and brought her back here, and they got married.'

John was studiedly staring at the table, his shoulders shaking imperceptibly. Mark encouraged his mother to carry on. 'The reverend married a prostitute?' he asked. Fran blushed. 'She might have been, she was certainly in the company of that sort of woman, but we don't say that, do we? Anyway, she was from a good family. Sadly, after their son was born, she ran away. Arthur went to look for her again, but she didn't want to be found. So poor little Alexander was raised mostly by his aunties and uncles, just like Arthur had been.'

'We know Xan,' Mark offered. 'He's in maths and music with me.'

Fran brightened up. 'He'll be at Helen Townsend's party, then?'

'Yup,' John said. 'Andy Ransome too, probably.'

'Well, it's nice to know that you're mixing with a better sort, at last! Do you think young Xan will enter the Church too?'

The boys exchanged a glance. 'No, not really Mum,' Mark said, at last.

'Well, I'll drive you there and pick you up afterwards. Will the reverend be there?'

'No, just people from school, but we're all pretty sensible.' Mark said. 'We'll get a taxi home; I don't want you to stay up.'

'I won't. I'll pick you up at ten.'

John choked. 'Auntie Fran, please! You'll make us look stupid. I'm nearly seventeen; can't we stay until midnight, at least?'

Frannie's eyes grew misty, and she swallowed hard. 'I forget how fast you're growing up. Your fathers took me and Miriam out to a party on my seventeenth birthday and my dad let us all stay out until after midnight. That's when Anthony proposed to me.'

Mark blushed; his mother rarely spoke about his father. He got his voice under enough control to say, 'Well, I don't think we'll be proposing to anyone. But please can we stay out?'

Frannie nodded. 'Have you got enough money?'

The boys nodded, but she picked up her purse anyway and gave each of them five pounds. 'In case of emergency,' she said. It went unsaid that they were to give it back if they didn't need it.

John finished his meal and nipped out to the mini-market, coming back with twelve cans of Breaker and a bottle of red wine. Frannie rolled her eyes, but said nothing.

Frannie dropped them off at the end of the drive and they stepped through the open front door. Helen was in the hall with a couple of nervously giggling girls from the maths class. Mark greeted them, and John wandered into the kitchen to find a corkscrew, coming back with drinks and handing them round casually. Within minutes he was in the living room, chatting and choosing records to play. Mark stared at him, wondering how anyone could be so effortlessly sociable. He opened a can of Breaker and played with the ring pull for a while, looking at Helen nervously.

'You can leave your jacket upstairs if you want, in one of the bedrooms,' she suggested. He seized the chance to break the awkward silence and made his way upstairs. One of the bedroom doors was ajar, and he could see a pile of coats already on the big double bed. He threw his jacket on the pile and heard a muffled giggle. Embarrassed, he turned away, but stopped when a deep voice said, 'If that's a girl, don't go,' followed by another, instantly recognisable voice saying, 'I don't care what sex it is.'

A long arm reached from the bed and turned the lamp on. Mark stared at Xan and Andy, naked and aroused in each other's arms. He breathed faster for a moment, then turned and left, running down the stairs. Helen was waiting in the hall. He glared at her. 'You knew! You knew they were in there.'

'Bad boys, the pair of them.' She laughed. 'Does it bother you?'

'I don't like being messed with,' he whispered, and walked away, looking for somewhere quiet. His mind was a whirl of images: hard, tanned bodies pressed against each other, Xan's hand caressing… He shut his eyes, but that made things worse: the images came to life. He found the kitchen, where he drank some cold water, before going through to the living room and staring at John until he got the message and walked over.

'I just saw Ransome and Kendrick shagging,' Mark breathed.

'Shagging who?' John asked, interested.

'Each other.' Mark said, looking directly at his cousin.

John's eyes widened. 'I *knew* there was something going on there.'

'John, they asked me to join them! Do I look gay to you?'

John looked at his cousin carefully, and Mark rolled his eyes. John nodded.

'Do you want me to beat them up?' he asked.

Mark looked at his cousin hopelessly. 'Why? Why would I want that?'

''Cos they were teasing you?' John said carefully.

'I don't need protecting,' Mark snarled. 'I'm a bloody werewolf, in case you'd forgotten.'

John laughed. 'Yeah, sorry. So, the question is, where does Helen fit in with them? It seems like such a waste. She's fit.'

Mark shrugged. 'I don't particularly care, it's all bloody weird. I'm not sure if I want to get any more involved with this lot than we already are.'

John glanced back at the girls on the sofa. 'Look, Mark, I'm getting on really well with these two, come and join me, let's see if we can break your duck.'

The younger boy looked at the girls, both of

them slightly plump, curvy, with short, dark hair and flicked, bleached fringes. 'No thanks, not my type,' he muttered.

'Jeez, when you want tail, you really want tail, don't you?' John joked, and Mark turned away, trying to be annoyed, but failing. John always managed to cheer him up. He wandered back to the kitchen, finding Helen again and glaring at her silently.

'We're three couples,' she volunteered, quietly.

'Huh?' Mark asked.

'You were wondering, weren't you? We're not a threesome, we never all do it together. We're three couples – me and Xan, Xan and Andy, me and Andy.'

'OK.' Mark clipped his words, wondering where she was going with this.

'And it gets worse. We're cousins. Andy's mum is my dad's first cousin. Xan's dad is their second cousin. We grew up together, same age, no brothers or sisters, always together. Anyway, don't be scared of them; they're harmless…'

He shrugged and opened another beer.

'They wanted me to join them,' he whispered.

'Xan said that?' She laughed, a little nervously. 'Look, it's not what you think, Xan's a bit of a flirt, that's all.'

Mark stayed silent. He felt naïve, innocent, left behind as these people his own age lost themselves in a world he felt he could never join.

Helen kissed him lightly on the forehead. 'I really like you, Mark.'

Mark closed his eyes, embarrassed. 'I'm not really into girls,' he whispered. 'Or boys,' he added, quickly.

Helen's laugh was rich and kind. 'Oh, I wasn't coming on to you! I meant that I think you're interesting.'

Andy wandered in, fully dressed, looking relaxed and cheerful. 'Hey, Mark. You OK?' He didn't meet Mark's eyes, and the dark-haired boy understood that the big blond didn't want to discuss what had just happened. That was fine; Mark would be happy to sweep it under the carpet. Andy picked up a can of Breaker, looking at it carefully. 'Loony juice! Who brought this?' he asked, before cracking it open and taking a swig.

'Big John.' Helen laughed, and Andy smirked. 'How many hearts has he broken so far?' he asked.

Mark suddenly understood that his presence here was no casual invitation; these rich kids were as fascinated by him and John as the Prestons were by them. Andy had his arm round Helen now, and there was something protective in his stance that struck Mark as adult and natural. He was already beginning to realise that Helen was someone he could respect, and perhaps he should reconsider his views on her loud friends. Xan had sneaked in at some point and was drinking something clear and viscous from a tumbler. The thin blond laughed. 'Poteen … Hel's dad brought it back from Ireland, it's strong stuff.'

Mark refused a glass; the Breaker was already making him a little dizzy and he had a good reason to fear losing control. He realised that Andy had taken hold of his arm and wanted his attention. He glanced around, and everyone seemed to be cool, so he followed the big blond into another bedroom. It was a teenager's room, with posters on the wall, large cupboards, a guitar on an expensive-looking stand and a small drum kit against the wall. Unbidden, he picked up the guitar, examining it carefully. 'She's gorgeous,' he breathed.

Andy looked pleased and proud. 'My birthday present, two years ago. I've got others, but I leave this one here at Hel's. This is our band room – Hel's mum and dad are cool with it. Xan drums, Hel sings and strums a bit. We were thinking of getting a band together, and wondered if you'd be interested.'

'I'm with John.' Mark said shortly.

'Yeah, we know.' Andy smiled. 'He's invited too. You've both got the right look for a proper rock band.'

'John's a singer, you know? Where do I fit in?'

We thought he could play bass, and you could be the rhythm…?'

Mark looked at Andy and laughed. 'You want us to fill out your rich-kid band? No thanks.' He didn't drop the guitar, though; his fingers slid over it, exploring it carefully before playing a single note, making tiny adjustments as he went.

Andy went quiet. 'What are you doing?'

'Tuning it.'

'You've not heard it yet,' Andy complained.

'I can feel it … how tight the strings are, the action … everything works together.' He smiled and strummed a chord, winced theatrically, made another tiny adjustment and strummed it again, this time relaxing and smiling, satisfied. Andy laughed.

'You're joking, right? It was fine the first time.'

Mark shrugged. 'If you say so, she's your guitar.'

'What else do you play?'

'What have you got?'

Andy grinned and opened a cupboard. It held more instruments than Mark had ever seen together before. He drew out a ukulele. Mark looked at it carefully.

'I've never held one of these before,' he said, strumming at it experimentally. 'It's cute.'

'You can have it, if you want. My cousin gave it to me last month, but I don't really want it.'

'Xan?'

'No, Ronnie. He's a lot older than us, he works for my dad. He's my mum's cousin really. You probably saw him this afternoon when he took Helen to the market…?'

'Ah. Another cousin. I thought he was her boyfriend.'

'Get off!' Andy laughed. 'He's fucking ancient.'

Mark turned the uke over in his hands. 'I

can't accept this,' he said reluctantly. 'It's old, it might be valuable.'

Andy shrugged and took it away, putting it on a shelf.

'OK, fair enough,' he said picking up the guitar. 'Get thee on those drums, lad,' he said, and Mark laughed and sat himself down, experimenting with the set-up. 'I've only ever played bongos at school,' he confessed, trying to work out what the pedals did. The crashing and banging summoned a blond sprite into the room who stood with his arms folded, watching Mark with a critical eye.

Mark ignored Xan. These weren't Xan's drums, they were Helen's, here for the fun of her guests, and he was Helen's guest, for tonight. He was still experimenting when a cool hand took his wrists, guiding his fingers into a more comfortable grip around the sticks and bringing his shoulders and hips into a position that gave him better access to the pedals and the cymbals. There was a sudden jolt as the stool dropped a couple of inches. Xan licked his lips.

'Better, honey?' he asked. Mark flushed; whatever Hel said, this boy unnerved him.

'Yeah, thanks,' he said, looking away quickly and checking Andy's face to see if he was being laughed at. Andy was completely serious, watching Mark with an expression that was already familiar to him. It was the same expression John used when he was waiting to take his cue from Mark. Mark started to lay down a beat, progressing round it and clumsily trying to bring in the cymbals and the pedals, frustrated already by his own lack of ability. Xan was grinning from ear to ear, and gestured for him to get off the stool, slipping into his place, and magically playing, perfectly, the percussion that had been imprisoned in Mark's head only minutes ago. Andy soberly handed him the guitar, and wandered out, leaving Xan and Mark jamming together, intuitive to each other already. Andy returned with a new-looking bass guitar, tuned it, and found a quirky bass line that fitted in with what they were doing. Mark was aware that the three of them were making a lot of noise, and wasn't surprised when John followed Helen into the room. Helen started to croon gently; she had a sweet voice, and she was singing some poem by William Blake, fitting the words to Mark's melody. John caught on, harmonising with her. She looked at him in shocked wonder and fell silent, allowing him to find his full voice, louder and stronger and more confident with each passing line. They came to an end and stared at each other.

'I resign. I'll manage you or something.' Helen laughed.

'Oh, that was better than sex,' Xan breathed. 'Thank you, Mark, I'll be daydreaming about that for weeks.'

Mark blushed again, and John nudged him. 'They're not bad,' he muttered.

'*We're* not bad,' Mark confirmed. 'Band practice on Monday night OK?'

John grinned. 'The John Preston Band!'

Xan scowled. 'Kendrick's Koven, obviously.'

Andy folded his arms. 'Ransome's Hearts,' he suggested. 'Or I refuse to settle for bass.'

'The Ransomed Hearts?' Helen said quietly. They looked at each other and laughed.

'The Ransomed Hearts,' Mark confirmed, caressing the guitar before carefully placing it on its stand. He left the room, his heart suddenly full.

Chapter 7

Sixth form had come and gone, A levels had been revised for and taken, and now it was time for the results.

Five envelopes on the kitchen table, untouched. Helen, John, Andy and Mark had taken the four chairs. Xan stood behind Helen, his hand on her shoulder.

'Who goes first?' he asked.

'All together,' Helen said. 'It's the only fair way.'

'OK then, quick, before my mum gets home,' Mark said. 'She was bad enough when the O level results came out. We need to make our decisions before we speak to our parents.' He shrugged. 'Don't we?'

'Yeah.' Andy nodded. 'OK, on three.' He counted down, and the five of them opened their envelopes together.

Helen cleared her throat. 'Three As: biology, chem and maths. C in music. Shit.'

'Three As is brilliant,' Mark said quickly. 'And you don't need music for uni, do you?'

'I thought I deserved a B, but never mind. I'll get over it.' Helen forced a smile. 'And I'm happy with the As, of course I am. OK, who's next?'

Mark looked at his friends. 'Two As: music and maths. Bs in general studies and English.'

Helen smiled. 'Well done. It can't have been easy, having to work on Saturdays and doing the band stuff too…'

John yawned and waved his results slip. 'I got an A in Spanish! Look!' He laughed. 'I was only taking it as a joke. Oh, B in music, Cs in geography and general studies.'

'That'll get you into uni, if that's what you want,' Helen murmured. 'Andy?'

'Straight Bs.' He shrugged. 'That's OK, Cambridge gave me an unconditional offer anyway.'

Xan rolled his eyes. 'Ah, the golden boy. It's not what you know…'

Andy scowled. 'I'm not going anyway. Am I? Are we? Xan?'

Xan laid his results slip on the table like a winning poker hand. 'Straight As. That'll get me to Durham or Manchester for physics, if that's what I want. I'm not touching Oxford or Cambridge with a bargepole.'

'My clever boy,' Helen said quietly. Mark glanced at her suspiciously but she wasn't being sarcastic. She looked genuinely happy.

'So?' Xan looked round at his friends. 'What now? I mean, we've been talking about whether we go our separate ways to uni, and we can keep the band together during the hols…'

'Might work for me and thee, cousin dear,' Andy said, 'but we all know that Mark and John have both applied to Liverpool and they'll be in some student band together by the middle of the first term. They won't be able to help themselves, and then we're out in the cold.'

'Except that we've got something special with the Hearts.' Mark bit his lip. 'I don't want to break up.'

'Fuck that, I don't even want to go to uni,' John muttered.

'Just to clarify, I do. I've got a place at Leicester, biochemistry. I can still manage you part-time, get involved in Rock Soc or Ents or whatever, that'll help.' Helen shrugged. 'If you stay together.'

Xan smiled at her. 'The way I see it, I can be an amazingly brilliant rock star, or an amazingly brilliant physicist. To be honest, both sound like lots of fun. I don't need to worry about money, I've got a trust fund from my grandparents. Helen's already got part of her inheritance, and Andy's parents are richer than anyone has a right to be.'

'Doesn't mean that *I* have any money,' Andy pointed out. 'And if I tell Mum and Dad that I'm not going to Cambridge, they'll have a fit.'

'Tell 'em you're deferring, having a gap year,' Xan said.

'Yeah, they'll go for that if I travel, or intern with a Ransome Industries department, but the band … not sure they'll go for it. Mark, what about your mum?'

'Haven't talked about it. She's thrilled that John and I have lots of options. She didn't go to uni herself, nor did John's mother. I don't know what she'll say.'

'Deferral. I keep telling you. Any fuss, just say it's one year, to get the band out of your system so you can concentrate on uni next year. Promise 'em a goal for the band … a single, breaking even with band costs, whatever.' Xan grinned.

'You'd be bored stiff in academia,' John sighed. 'You get twitchy if you're away from a drum kit for more than three days.'

Mark spoke up. 'John and I will have to get jobs. Something that doesn't interfere with evening practice and weekend gigs. I mean, if we decide to do the band, not uni.'

'Oh god, us too,' Andy said. 'Whatever happens, my dad won't put up with me not working. And that goes for Xan too. Sorry, mate, but you know my dad, if you're not gainfully employed he'll take it out on me.' He looked round the table. 'We seem to be talking about the band, not about uni.'

'Yeah.' Mark stood up. 'Anyone fancy a cuppa?'

They met again, four days later, in the same place.

'Helen sends her apologies. She's decided that it's definitely uni for her, so she's gone to Lancaster to get some textbooks. Swot.' Xan grinned. 'She's so excited.' He looked round. 'So, what's happening?'

Mark shrugged. 'I mentioned deferring. My mum just shook her head and told me to make my mind up. I told her that I wanted to keep the band going. John said the same. She said she'd help us keep the books, which means that she'll know if we're spending more money on it than we're making. We have to get proper jobs too, until the band is making enough for us to live on. What about you?' He bit his lip. 'I mean, John and me, we could do it alone, or get another drummer, but…'

Xan grinned. 'Don't be daft, I'm in. My father has disowned me, but Helen's mum and dad have given me a roof over my head. Not that it makes much difference, they pretty much brought me up, it's just official now.'

Mark shook his head. 'I'm sorry, Xan. If I'd known I would never have …'

'Not your fault, mate. My father has been disapproving of me for years, this is just him grabbing a good excuse to not have me around. No big deal – I never liked him anyway.'

Andy spoke firmly. 'Xan will be fine. As for me, if anyone's interested, I've spent the last four days in intense negotiations with my parents. They want me to learn the business, which involves working in different companies at the ground floor, nine to five. I'll get paid the going rate, they'll keep a roof over my head and I've said that I'll sit down with dad at least once a month to review stuff. Other than that, my time is my own, and if I want to play in a rock band evenings and weekends, that's up to me. Dad said that Cambridge is all about making connections, and I can do that at work, and in the band. He'll introduce me to people anyway.'

Mark frowned. 'So the band is your hobby?'

Andy shook his head, blond curls flaring out as he did so. 'No. My dad might think that's the deal, but I'm in. OK, I have a hell of a lot to fall back on if we fail, but we won't fail. We've got bookings from school and college friends until the end of September, so it's time to let people know that we're here to stay.' He reached into a bag and took out a bottle of champagne and four paper cups. He poured the drinks and passed them round. 'A toast: to the future, to the Hearts.'

'To the future, to the Hearts,' came the echo, from Xan, from Mark, and from John.

Chapter 8

The rain had been threatening all day, and now it came, dropping from the sky in cool sheets. Mark raised his face and let the rain rinse the sweat away, he was drenched to the skin in seconds, and relished the change in temperature. The pub had been packed out, and towards the end of the gig the heat had been almost unbearable, bodies packed tight in front of the stage, the vibe unmistakable. He stole another moment to remember the faces of the crowd, contorted with hunger for the music that only the Ransomed Hearts could supply. The crowd in this town was ready for a move to a bigger venue, and he made a mental note to research possibilities – and soon, before the buzz died down too much. It had taken six years of hard gigging to get the band to this stage, and none of them were getting any younger. Andy's parents were putting more and more pressure on him to quit the band and move into the family business.

Mark checked that the back doors of the van were firmly locked and went back to the pub. The pub managers, Deirdre and Mick, a pair of rock fans of 1960s vintage, were regaling John with stories about the festivals and concerts of their youth. The front doors were closed, and the shutters down. Mark was still hyped up from the gig. He accepted a pint of blackcurrant and soda, and took a seat next to his cousin.

John shifted a little to make room and looked at him. 'I was wrong, you're not too thin to get wet in a rainstorm,' he joked. 'Ladies and gentlemen, I present the winner of tonight's wet T-shirt competition, Mr Mark Preston, the greatest guitarist Hull has ever seen.'

'The greatest white-van man too.' Mark pointed out. 'I thought you were going to help me with the gear?'

'Whoops.' John's expression was so contrite and mournful that Mark instantly forgave him. 'I thought Andy and Xan were helping you,' John said.

Mark looked across at the bar, where their tour manager, Helen, was counting the takings from the merchandise stall and the door. She waved at him and wandered over.

'Where are my boys?' she asked.

'Last time I saw them they were getting some fresh air and talking to fans,' he said. 'Do you want me to get them?'

'Good grief, no, I'll go and round them up. Did they let you load the gear all by yourself? They're bad, the pair of them.' She sounded quite unconcerned. 'John? Are you coming clubbing later with me and the boys?'

John looked up, pushing his dark curls away from his face. 'Mark? Are you coming?'

The guitarist shook his head and made his excuses. 'I want to get an early night; it's a long drive to Wolverhampton tomorrow. You guys have fun.' The weight of the day had hit him suddenly, and he fought against a yawn. Deirdre was smiling at him fondly. 'Thanks for coming up here, you lot are real favourites. Shall we pencil in another date?'

He shifted a little; he should have expected this. The upstairs room of the pub had a capacity of a hundred, and he knew for a fact that they'd squeezed in more than that. He was searching for the words when Deirdre helped him out.

'Mark, hon, it's OK. I can see where you guys are going, and all I ask is that you remember us when you're big. You've worked hard for this for a hell of a long time, I know. Send us a signed CD or two for the Christmas raffle or something.' She reached out in a motherly way and tucked a stray lock of hair behind his ear. 'I know the guy who books bands for a rock club in town – it's five-hundred capacity, but I reckon you could fill if it you get the publicity right. Shall I give you the number? Just mention my name when you ring him.'

John, who had been listening in, whooped with glee and enveloped Deidre in a bear hug that knocked the breath out of her.

'DeeDee, you're an angel,' he yelled. 'I'm off, where's this club? Is it open tonight? I might as well scope it out while we're here.'

Deirdre gave him directions and called a cab. Mark wandered out and walked to the van. He could see Andy and Hel leaning against the wall, deep in conversation, and he held back from interrupting, contenting himself with a brief wave as he passed them. Helen turned as he drove past, and he didn't see her face. They were all staying in a motel a couple of miles from the pub, and had downstairs rooms next to the car park. He managed to park the hired van less than twenty yards from his bedroom window; if he slept with the window slightly open there was no chance it would be nicked – his reactions were too good for that. He left the bedroom door unlocked as he wasn't sure when the others would get back. It was still stupidly hot and he treated himself to a cold shower. He stripped the blankets from one of the twin beds and slipped between the sheets. The clock said that it was late, and the hotel was quiet. He wondered briefly what his friends were doing and smiled to himself. Whatever it was, they would have more fun without him. John had a habit of acting like a big brother when they went to clubs together, continually wandering over to check if he was OK. Really, it was better if he just got some rest.

His head was buzzing with excitement, though; he was tired, but there was too much to think about. This felt like 'it', like the breakthrough they'd been working towards for so many years. They'd achieved some sort of critical mass that night, the audience had left knowing that they'd been part of something special, and Hel had been busy to the last, selling cassettes, T-shirts and badges to an eager crowd. Mark had fled to the van to avoid a girl who had been staring at him with a predatory interest all night. He'd sat on the wheel arch, in the dark, alone, until he was sure she was gone. He giggled at the thought, seeing the funny side. He was aroused by the success of the gig, and by the thought of that girl, who'd clearly wanted him, but he deliberately turned his thoughts away from the erotic. Still a virgin, in his twenties, he found the idea of masturbating in a strange bed repulsive; he'd wait until he got home, where everything was familiar, and relieve the tension with his favourite fantasy, which involved running through the woods, chasing a shadowy figure, a naked girl who could almost outrun him, who would surrender herself to him under cool moonlight, giving her body and soul to him forever. His fantasy involved waking up to find her gone, the shape of her body in the fallen leaves replaced by the imprint of a sleeping wolf, of finding scraps of fur clinging to low-lying branches. He would sit up and wait, and the girl would come back, and tease him into Changing, because she would know what he was, and she would love him for it.

He smiled cynically. 'And then, Mark, they all lived happily ever after,' he muttered. He wasn't doing himself any favours and he rolled on to his stomach, cuddling the pillow. His ears still rang, but the effects of the gig were fading, and he knew he'd be asleep soon.

He was drifting off when there was a sharp knock on the door.

'Who?' he muttered.

'It's Hel. Can I come in?'

'Er, yeah, sure,' he replied, switching on the bedside light and sitting up. He reached down and pulled a blanket over himself as Helen let herself into the room. She looked troubled.

'Sorry for waking you up. I just wanted to give you the key for my room. The merch is in there, I've just brought it up from the car. I don't know if there'll be room for it in the van, but I'm sure you'll sort something out.' Her voice was very carefully controlled, and he peered at her.

'Hel, what's up?'

'I'm afraid you'll have to find someone else to look after you. I just can't deal with Xan any more.'

Mark blinked. 'What's he done?'

She shrugged. 'He's fucked off somewhere with some boy from the crowd. It's not the sleeping around that bothers me, it's the lack of consideration. He was the one who suggested that we go out after the gig. *We*, as in me and him. He didn't even come back into the pub to tell me that he'd pulled – Andy had to tell me.'

'So why didn't you go clubbing with Andy?' Mark asked cautiously. Helen shook her head. 'That's *not* the fucking point. Sorry Mark, but I'm tired of me and Andy consoling each other whenever Xan lets us down. I need to get away from this whole situation and just be myself for a while. I've been part of this merry trio since I was … well, too young to be admitting to, really.' She pulled a face. 'Besides, I wasn't in any mood for fun, after that. John and Andy have gone out together, and here I am.'

Their eyes met, and Mark saw a flicker of possibility in Helen's eyes, but she blinked and it was gone. 'Here I am. I'm really sorry to let you down, I hope things work out for you, and that Xan learns how to stop being an arse.' She swallowed hard and took a ring off her finger, leaning over to take an envelope from a drawer. 'Give this to Xan, will you? It belonged to our mutual great-great-grandmother. I think he only proposed to me to keep it in the family.'

She handed him the ring in the envelope, unsealed, and he put it in the drawer next to his bed.

'Hel … this feels wrong; you're a part of this.'

'No, I'm not. I'm playing at being a rock chick when I should be looking for a job or a PhD project. Looking after you as a part-time thing when I was a student was fun, but I have no idea what made me think I wanted to make a career out of looking after a gang of overgrown boys. Present company excepted – you're the only one with any sense.' She favoured him with a sudden brilliant smile and he returned it cautiously. She bent to kiss him on the forehead.

'Be lucky, Mark. You've got real talent, don't waste it.' She left the room and he groaned and switched the light off.

Within a minute, he heard her start up her car and drive away. She must have had the windows open, because he heard the first few notes of their second album, then silence. 'Fuck. Fuck the fucking fuckers, everything is fucked,' he whispered.

He awoke at four, hearing John's voice as a taxi dropped him off outside the hotel. He sat up again, frowning, as John tapped on the window.

'Use the frigging door,' Mark said, trying to keep his voice low. John started to explain, much too loud, about losing his key, and in the end it was easier to simply open the window and drag his cousin into the room. John grinned deliriously, fell on to the other bed and was snoring within a minute. Mark gave up on sleep and started to pack.

He was the only one up at breakfast. There was no sign of Andy or Xan, and John was still sound asleep when he got back to the room. Mark let him sleep, they going nowhere until the others turned up, and they had three hours until they had to check out. He opened the curtains and peered out at the van. Untouched, safe; all their precious gear stowed away.

Behind him, there was an insistent rap on the door. Andy strode in, looking none the worse for wear. He cast a half-amused look at John, who was still sleeping.

'No stamina, that lad,' he commented. 'Where's our Hel?'

Mark shook his head. 'Gone. Where've you been?'

'Where haven't I been? We went to that club that DeeDee mentioned – it's ideal for us. There was a band on, girl singer…' He grinned. 'Very, very cute, fantastic vocal cords.' He looked around. 'What do you mean, "gone".'

'I don't know where to, but last night she resigned as tour manager, drove off and left her engagement ring behind.' Mark kept his tone neutral.

Andy sat down heavily on John's bed, ignoring the protests from the hungover singer, who was beginning to struggle to consciousness.

'Is this because of that boy that Xan went off with? If I'd known she was that upset I would have stayed with her.' Andy was frowning. 'I'll ring her. She should be home by now.' He picked up the hotel phone and asked for an outside line. Mark sat quietly, listening to Andy as he tried to persuade Helen to come back. He hung up, baffled. 'She doesn't seem angry, but she's not budging. I think she means it.' He spun the ring on his little finger then handed it back to Mark. 'It's just as much her ring as it is mine or Xan's. It was left to us jointly. Our great-gran had a wicked sense of humour. It's worth a bit.' He brightened up. 'We'll pay a couple of fans to run the merch stall, and I can do the bookings for now. It's not as if we'll never see her again – it's my gran's birthday in three weeks, she'll have to be there.'

He was interrupted by a groan from John. 'Mark? Mark? Are you there?'

'Yeah.'

'Then I'm not in hell,' John moaned. ''Cos you're bound for paradise, you celibate fucker.'

Mark giggled, despite everything. 'Celibate fucker?' he asked.

'Shut up and run me a bath, and find me some food, and some clothes that don't stink.'

'Yes, master.' Mark grinned. 'And then what? Shall I bring you wine, women and song?'

'Fuck no, that's what nearly killed me. Toast and coffee…' John flung his arm across the bed dramatically. 'And perhaps eggs, sausage, bacon, tomatoes, beans, black pudding and … did I say eggs?'

Andy grinned. 'He'll live, let him run his own bath.'

John opened his eyes. 'Ransome, you bastard. You left me with that hen party. You callous son of a bitch.'

Andy nodded. 'I am. But you weren't complaining at the time.'

John shook his head, then reconsidered. He peered into his trousers. 'What happened to my kecks? Christ, what happened to my dick?' His face went a peculiar colour, and he made for the bathroom. He called out, relieved, 'It's OK, it's just lipstick.' He went quiet, and they heard him running a bath.

Mark rolled his eyes. 'And you wonder why Helen left? You three are like a bloody bad joke.'

John was calling for him, and Mark went into the bathroom. John was trying to peer over his shoulder into the mirror. Something was written on his back. Mark read it aloud: 'This boy is the property of Singleton and Partners Accountants. If found, please return to the personnel department.' He managed a smile. 'John, you're just a plaything to them.'

The singer mustered a smile. 'I know. It's great, I have no self-respect whatsoever. Did Andy score?'

'With the singer from the club,' Mark reported soberly. 'Look, shut up, we've got a big problem. Helen has left us.'

'She'll be back,' John said, with the supreme

confidence of someone who knows that problems get sorted around him. He stepped into the bath and submarined.

'Fuck,' Mark muttered as he left.

It was almost check-out time when Xan wandered in, hair carefully styled, make-up immaculate. Andy and John were outside, looking miserable and stowing the merchandise in the van. Mark was checking their room to make sure that nothing had been left behind when Xan pushed the door open, grinning from ear to ear.

'He makes me feel so young!' he declared, falling back on to John's bed. 'I think I'm in love.'

'That boy? If he's eighteen I'm a monkey's uncle.' Mark frowned. 'And I hate it when you shag the fans – it's bad PR. They get all involved, then upset, then we never see them again. Haven't you got a conscience?'

Xan grinned. 'A) I have condoms, they serve in lieu of a conscience. B) The girls are just as much fans as the boys, and you don't get snitty about them: I smell sexism, and maybe just a little homophobia.'

Mark dug into the pocket of his leather jacket. He handed the envelope to Xan. 'She's gone. I think she means it.'

Xan turned the ring over, studying it carefully, as if it held some clue to the way he suddenly felt. His eyes were wide and shocked when he finally looked at Mark.

'Helen wouldn't just leave. She's part of me.'

'I'd say she's got tired of that attitude,' Mark said. Xan was wilting by the second; he rolled off the bed and walked slowly to the bathroom. He was still there when Andy and John returned.

'He's back.' Mark pointed to the bathroom door. 'He's not taking it well.'

John was grumbling. 'That van is packed to the gills, and there's only room for three of us in the cab.'

Andy nodded. 'No problem, mate, Xan and I will train it to Wolverhampton. Mark, give us the address of the venue.'

Xan must have heard them; he emerged from the bathroom with his face streaked with tears. 'I'm not going. I've got to go home.'

Andy rolled his eyes. 'You fucking well *are*.' He pushed Xan back into the bathroom, and the dark-haired cousins waited outside, listening in unashamedly.

Andy's voice had dropped an octave, and he spoke with immense authority.

'Xan, this isn't a game. You promised that you'd stick at it. We're right on the edge of something big and we *cannot* cancel a gig now.'

'Andy, it's *Helen*!' Xan wailed.

'No, it's you. Helen's fine, I spoke to her earlier. She's had enough of us, for now, but if you really want to make her happy again, you'll give her reason to be proud of you. Are you listening?'

'Why's she mad at me?' Xan said, in a low voice.

'Perhaps because one minute you're talking

about getting married and having kids, and the next minute you're off over the horizon with some cute kid from the crowd?'

'Shit, she knows I can't do the fidelity thing,' he muttered.

'She wants honesty, and she doesn't want to be left outside some pub at midnight, wondering where the fuck you disappeared to. Pick up your bags, we're going too. You can ring her from the station.'

Xan looked chastened and Andy was pale as they emerged from the bathroom. 'We'll see the two of you later tonight, we'd better get going,' Xan said. 'Shit, who's gonna manage us?'

They all looked at Mark.

'Oh no. I'm not doing it. I'm crap at talking to strangers. Andy's good with people; he's a natural bossy git.'

Andy smiled. 'From a long line of bossy gits, to be fair. OK, I'll do the bookings and make sure we get paid, you do the admin and make sure we know where we're going.'

Mark picked up his bag and led the way out of the room. Behind him, Xan was walking slowly, toying with the antique diamond ring until Andy grabbed it off him.

'I'll look after that,' he said firmly. 'You'll just end up giving it to the first sweet thing to catch your eye.' Xan surrendered meekly.

Mark checked the back doors of the van again and got behind the wheel. 'You OK?' he asked John.

'Me? I'm fine, why shouldn't I be? It's a bummer about Helen. Do you think we'll see her again?'

Mark thought about it carefully. 'Yeah, I think we will.'

Chapter 9

Andy and Xan got out of the taxi and gazed up the long drive, taking in the number of cars parked there, and on the road outside. The big old house glowed in the light of the setting sun, the west wing duller, in the shadow of a looming cypress. The windows and doors were flung open, and music spilled out. Andy touched his hair self-consciously. 'How do I look?'

'Gorgeous, darling. How about me?' Xan was wearing black, including a black bandanna. He'd even dyed his hair black, and it framed his fragile features in delicate wisps.

Andy studied his cousin carefully. Xan had lost weight in the last three weeks, and he'd never been able to afford to do that; his jeans were supposed to be skintight, but they hung loosely at his hips. His T-shirt was just a little too small, exposing his pale, taut belly. But his arms were still muscular, and Andy felt a tiny erotic thrill as he resisted the impulse to stroke them.

'You're too thin,' he said. 'But Gran will sort that out. Come on, let's do it.'

Xan held back. 'Do you think Helen will be there?' he asked.

Andy took his hand. 'Of course she will, and she'll probably be wondering where we are.'

'I was, actually.' Helen's voice made them both jump. It came from behind a low hedge, and the young men peered over it. She was slouching on a bench, her legs crossed loosely at the ankles. She was dressed in a salmon-pink flapper dress and wore a silver tiara set with rubies.

Andy managed a smile. 'You've been in the dressing-up box again,' he accused.

'So has Alexander, from the look of things. What have you done to your hair?' She was keeping her voice light, but she couldn't tear her eyes away from Xan. Andy turned away a little; it had always been the same, he and Helen orbiting the same star, slaves to Xan's ever-changing moods. He turned too quickly when she touched his arm, drawing his attention back to her. She looked eerily beautiful in the half light of dusk: a ghostly echo of a long-ago celebration. She'd cut her hair too, in an asymmetrical bob that complemented her outfit. It suited her, emphasising her beauty in a way that the casual rock-chick look never had. She was smiling at him. 'Come on, both of you, escort me back to the house. I was getting tired of trying to explain that you hadn't arrived with me, so I came out to find you.'

Freshly raked gravel crunched under their feet as they approached the house. The double oak doors were wide open, and Andy realised that someone was playing the title song to *Oklahoma!* on the piano. He could hear his mother's merry voice, slightly off-key as always. The three of them stood for a moment in the big hallway, then joined hands and walked into the living room. There was a moment's hush before everyone started to talk again. Helen bowed.

'I found them,' she sang out, and was

answered by a gruff voice from the depths of an ancient armchair.

'About time too!' Andy's grandmother said. 'It's not a party until the young men arrive. Hell's bells, Alexander! What have you done to your hair? And you're far too thin, come to the table with me and have some cake.'

Andy glanced at Helen, and they shared a conspiratorial grin. He spied his parents, standing together by the window. They still looked as crazy about each other as always. He wandered over to join them. They drew him affectionately into their circle; like Xan and like Helen, he was an only child. His dad was asking him about the band, as always testing his commitment and enthusiasm for what they were doing. Once again, he was being reassured that there was a place in the family firm for him if he ever wanted to give up 'the rough life'.

'Helen's research assistantship sounds interesting,' his mother said.

Andy frowned. 'What? I didn't know about that.'

'Oh, she interviewed last week. It was a bit of luck really; the place had gone months ago, but the post-holder had to give it up, family issues. Helen had been ringing around the colleges for a while, and was in the right place at the right time.'

He summoned a smile. 'So, where will she be?'

'Oh, close to hand: Lancaster. It's in the biochemistry department.' His parents fell silent, and he realised that they were actually a little flummoxed themselves. He looked from one to the other. Eventually, his dad spoke.

'Er, we noticed that she's not wearing the ring any more. Is the wedding off?'

'I would say so, yes,' Andy said.

'They seem to be getting on well enough,' his father commented. Andy looked across the room. Xan had taken a plate of food to Helen and was sat at her feet, holding the plate for her. Andy laughed. 'He's such a show-off. He knows we're all watching them.'

'Where's the ring, Andrew?' said his dad, bringing him back to reality. 'I hope Xan's not given it away to some deadbeat.'

'I've got it, it's safe,' Andy confirmed.

'I mean, I hate to drone on, but it's an heirloom. It wasn't given to the three of you in order to see it disappear outside the family.'

Andy felt impatient. The ring was just a bit of metal and stone; the important thing was that Helen had rejected the life that he and Xan had chosen.

The party carried on until the small hours as he caught up with his grandparents' generation, a remarkably spry and active bunch of over-eighties who all wanted to talk to him. There were dozens of them: brothers, sisters and cousins. His parents' generation was smaller, the products of one- or two-children families. His mother and Helen's father were first cousins, second cousins to Xan's dad. Andy, Xan and Helen, still in their twenties, were the youngest in the family. He could sometimes feel a melancholy air at these family gatherings, especially when the old people had asked him when he was going to bring a new bride to the family; when the old wooden swing in the back garden was going to get used again. He was tired, and Xan was flirting with him, playing with his hair. 'Sleep with me tonight,' Xan was whispering. 'Sleep with me here.'

'Your father would kill us,' Andy whispered back. 'He's only just recovered from you getting engaged to Helen. You know he was going on about you ruining her life?'

'Oh, my father thinks I'm an abomination anyway, and who says he needs to know?'

Andy frowned. 'Xan, you'll find some way of making sure that he finds out. No, leave me alone, you'd be with Helen if she wasn't still pissed at you. I'm not in the mood to be second choice.' He looked at Xan, anxious not to have upset him. For the thousandth time he wondered why it was so important not to upset Xan. He looked around. Helen was playing chess with her grandmother. They were both drinking neat Scotch, and it sounded like the old lady was telling some raunchy story from the dim and distant past. Every so often, Helen glanced at him. They'd not spent any time together all evening, and to his eyes she was growing more beautiful and desirable by the minute. It had been months since they'd made love; she had tried to take the engagement to Xan seriously, and Andy missed her.

Xan was laughing. 'You don't want me

anyway, I can always tell. Oh well, I'm turning in. Goodnight, my love.'

Xan kissed him full on the mouth, then left, leaving him breathless. His kiss tasted of brandy and apples, hazelnuts and chocolate. He stood stock-still for a moment, aware that he was being watched. It was Xan's father, glaring at him with the utmost disapproval.

'Young libertines,' he was saying to one of his cousins, who dismissed his grumbling.

'Ah, leave them be, we were all the same at that age.'

'I damn well wasn't,' growled Arthur Kendrick.

Andy frowned, and felt a contrary desire for his distant cousin, almost giving way to the impulse to follow him up the stairs. Nobody else in the room was alone, and he wasn't in the mood to crash anyone else's conversation. He went outside to find the back garden more overgrown than he remembered, but he made himself comfortable on the old swing, wrapping the ropes around his arms and leaning back. For the second time that night, Helen surprised him, gently placing her tiara among his abundant blond curls.

'Andy Ransome, I'd kill for hair like yours,' she murmured, leaning forward to kiss him.

'Be careful what you wish for, I'll probably be bald by the time I'm forty,' he joked. 'Hey, congratulations on the job. Are you pleased?'

'Yes, on balance,' she said carefully. 'It depends.'

'On what?'

'On whether or not you two shut me out completely from now on.' There was a trace of anxiety in her voice, and Andy sat up, surprised.

'What do you mean?' he asked.

'You've got your band, and I don't want to be part of that. And I certainly don't want to be Xan's hanger-on, I deserve better. But … well, it's always been the three of us, and I miss that. It scares me that you'll find someone else and we'll grow apart. Andy, you're my closest friends.'

'Ah, Helen, it's not the same without you. Even Mark and John miss you,' he whispered. 'Did I tell you that you look like a vision from the past tonight? Some ethereal beauty come back to haunt this place.' He took her hand: unadorned, slim, pretty. On impulse he reached deep into his pocket and drew out the scrap of red silk in which he kept the heirloom ring. He kissed her and slipped the ring on to her finger, where it belonged, where it had always looked so right.

She studied it carefully, then looked up, her eyes bright in the moonlight. 'I can't wear this.'

'It's yours. Xan gave it to you, then I gave it to you. That means it's all yours now.'

'Does it mean anything, though?' she whispered. 'It's supposed to be given in love.'

'But it is, you know that.' Andy smiled. He looked at her again and realised what she was saying. He blushed to the tips of his toes. 'Oh,' he said. He hurriedly got off the swing and seated her on it. He dropped to one knee and took her hand in his.

'Helen Margaret Isabel Townsend, will you be my wife?' he asked formally, bowing his head a little, then looking up, a huge grin on his face.

'Andrew Daniel Ransome, yes, of course,' she said.

Their kiss was interrupted by an ironic slow handclap from somewhere above them. Xan stood on a small iron balcony on the first floor. 'Bravo, and about bloody time,' he stage-whispered. 'Now, my darlings, can we all get some sleep?'

Chapter 10

Xan walked through the back door of the bungalow and grabbed an apple from the fruit bowl on the table. Frannie, stood at the sink, turned and smiled. 'The boys are in the living room.'

'Pah, I came here to visit you, Auntie Fran. Nice house, by the way. Shame you have to share it with Mark.'

He was teasing, and she threw a tea towel at him. 'Dry these dishes with me and tell me what's happening. Is your dad pleased about how well the band is doing?'

'The reverend hasn't spoken to me for two years now, and don't ask me why, because you won't approve either.'

Frannie shook her head. 'No, I probably wouldn't, but …'

'But you love me as I am, and he wants a model son. No, strike that, he never wanted a son at all. I'm just an inconvenience and an embarrassment. He calls me an abomination, you know?'

'Yes, I know.' Frannie sighed. She'd tentatively tried to develop a friendship with Xan's father when the boys first got the band together, and at first he had welcomed her overtures, appreciating her faith and intelligence, but when she refused to agree with his attacks on his own son, his interest had cooled. They still spoke, she made a point of attending his services sometimes, and she did her best to be a link between father and son.

Xan was hard work, but he was also obviously loved by both Mark and John, and Frannie couldn't resist a motherless boy, especially one who had showered her with affection since the day they'd first met.

'Do you like the new house?' There was a slight note of anxiety in Xan's voice.

'Xan, it's fine. I was OK in the old house, but it's nice to have a proper garden and somewhere to park my car.' She laughed. 'It's nice to have a new car! Mark and John have been very generous.'

Xan carefully dried the mugs and put them away. 'As long as you're OK.'

'I am. Boys,' she called, 'Xan is here, are you ready?'

Mark and John sauntered into the kitchen, John carrying a gift-wrapped parcel and a huge card. All three of them kissed her on the forehead and said goodbye before leaving. She heard the cars move off and sat down at the kitchen table. The window looked out on to a well-kept cottage garden that was separated from the moors beyond by a low stone wall. The bungalow stood alone, a quarter of a mile from the nearest neighbours; not exactly what she would have chosen, but Mark liked it. Frannie had enjoyed living in a busy town; her clients were nearby and it was easy to nip to the shops. But this was the house that Mark wanted. She supposed that she should be grateful that he didn't expect her to keep chickens or grow her own food. That kind of hard work could stay in the past.

The lads were on their way to Andy Ransome's birthday party. The big family party that the Ransomes had wanted to throw for his twenty-fifth hadn't happened because a big tour had got in the way, so they were celebrating his twenty-sixth. Frannie picked up the invitation from the table and smiled. She liked Andy's parents and Helen's mum well enough, but their lives were so far removed from hers that she rarely accepted their invitations.

The boys got back just after midnight, waking her up. She wrapped up in her dressing gown and went into the living room. 'I thought you were staying?' she said.

'Oh, the party was packed, we let someone else take the rooms,' Mark replied. 'Xan can have John's room and John can bunk in with me. Is that OK?'

'Just be quiet then.' Frannie went back to bed and fell straight asleep.

At 6 am, she woke again. Xan was shouting, and sounded distraught. She heard Mark speaking fast, and John's low voice, insistent and uncharacteristically angry. She switched on the light, and the boys fell silent. Mark came into the room.

'It's OK, Mum, just Xan being daft. Go back to sleep.'

'Did someone upset him? At the party?'

'He's fine, just a misunderstanding. We'll take him home.'

She shook her head and decided to go back to bed for another precious hour.

It had been a family party, with Helen and Andy the centre of attention. Mark and John had taken an early cue to leave, and Xan had decided to follow them. He parked up outside Mark's house and knocked quietly on the kitchen door just as Mark was starting to lock it. John raised his eyebrows and reached into the fridge for beer. 'Aren't you going home?' Mark asked. Xan shrugged. 'It's another half-hour's drive, and I'm sleepy. Can I stop over?'

Mark glanced at John, who shrugged and opened the beer, passing it to Xan. 'Don't see why not. I'll bunk in with Mark, you have my room.' They'd obviously woken Auntie Fran, who came into the kitchen to check on them. When she left, Mark smiled. 'Keep it quiet, eh? Let her sleep.' They chatted about the party for half an hour, and discussed an invitation for a radio gig, then John yawned theatrically and went to bed. Xan went to the car for his overnight bag, and when he got back, Mark was gone. The house was dead quiet. He found himself wondering, as always, about the intense relationship between John and Mark. They were definitely not lovers – he'd know if they were – and even he was squeamish at that thought as they were practically brothers. But their bond was closer than that; they shared something that Xan was excluded from, and Xan was very good at sniffing out exclusion. He brushed his teeth and went to bed as quietly as possible. He left the curtains open as his room was at the back of the house, with a view of nothing but the moonlit fells. John and Mark, in the next room, were silent.

He lay awake, restless. Perhaps he should

have gone home; he'd got a vibe from the Prestons that they wanted some time alone. They'd all been friends for so long, at sixth form, on the road, making music and now, making money, and there shouldn't really be anything that he didn't know about them. But there was a crawling, cold sense at the back of his mind that they had a secret and he wasn't part of it. He hugged the pillow and tried to sleep; he hated sleeping alone.

Early in the morning he woke with a start. He'd been dreaming about his own house on the lake, that he'd left the doors open, that there was danger. He opened his eyes and walked to the window. He saw shadows in the garden and was about to raise the alarm when he realised it was Mark and John. They were naked, in the cold night, and walking towards the wall at the end of the garden. Mark glanced at the house and Xan took a step back into the darkness of the room. The Prestons vaulted over the wall and walked towards the dark hills.

Xan dressed quickly and crept out of the house via the front door. He walked along the road and turned down a path that led in the direction that Mark and John had taken. He moved fast; he needed to know what was happening. He needed to be part of it.

Ten minutes took him to a shallow dip, unseen from the road and houses, and sheltered from the top of the hills by a steep cliff. He looked around, thinking that two pale bodies would be obvious in the moonlight, but could see nothing. A shadow in front of him moved, and he heard a low growl behind him. He swallowed hard and turned round. A huge black wolf stood behind him, head down, teeth bared. He took a step back, his legs weak with fear, and fell. He felt hot breath against his throat and looked into wild yellow eyes. There was a dark intelligence there, an intensity that he recognised instantly. He whispered, 'Mark?'

The wolves backed off and melted into the darkness. Xan scrambled to his feet, found the path and walked fast – he ran. He knew exactly where his coat was and he was going to grab it, get in his car, and drive back to Andy's parents' house and tell Andy what he'd seen. Then they would … he shook his head. He couldn't work out what he wanted to happen next. What had he seen, really? Two big dogs in a field at night. He remembered that look, that recognition, and he ran faster. He got to the bungalow and quietly let himself in through the front door. His car keys weren't in his coat pocket and he cursed, remembering that he'd left them in the kitchen. He pushed the kitchen door open quietly, and stopped dead. Mark and John were sat at the table, dressed in jeans and sweaters. Mark was holding Xan's car keys.

'What are you doing up in the middle of the night?' Mark asked.

Xan swallowed. These were his closest friends, but they were looking at him with a deep distrust. 'Just out for a walk,' he muttered. 'Couldn't sleep. I think I'll go home.'

John cleared his throat. 'You look a bit

shook up, mate. Are you OK to drive? I can drive you home, Mark can follow and bring me back.'

Xan shivered. Just how well did he know these men? 'I saw something,' he ventured.

'Yes?' Mark held his gaze.

'There aren't any wolves in England,' Xan said, his voice louder than he expected. 'But I saw two, on the hill. I followed you, and I couldn't find you, but I saw two wolves.'

They heard a light switch click in Frannie's bedroom and the sound of her moving around.

'You've woken my mum up,' Mark growled. He left the kitchen and Xan stayed silent, looking at John.

Mark came back. 'OK, Xan, there're no wolves in England, so what do you think you saw?'

Xan closed his eyes. 'You. I saw you.'

He trembled as John took hold of his arm. 'Don't freak out, mate. It's OK. We'll talk at your place. Auntie Fran doesn't know, and she doesn't need to.'

Xan's eyes widened. 'So it's true?'

'Hush. Get in your car, Mark will drive – you're in shock.' John guided Xan to the back seat and sat next to him. Mark drove, and in twenty minutes they were at Xan's new lakeside home.

Xan realised that he was even further from help than he had been at Mark's house, and he resisted as John helped him out of the car. 'No, no. I won't tell, I promise. No.'

'Fucksake man, it's me. I'm not going to eat you. Get out.'

John glanced at Mark, who stepped forwards. 'Xan, you're safe. It's us. We just want to talk. Let's go in, it's cold out here.'

Mark made some strong tea and poured sugar into Xan's. They sat down in the living room, and Mark coughed.

'OK, it's a secret. You get that? You can't tell anyone. God only knows what would happen to us if people found out. Medical experiments on us, on Mum too, probably. You can say goodbye to the band, that's for certain.'

John leaned forwards. 'Questions?'

Xan shook his head. 'So many. Does Andy know?'

Mark's eyes opened very wide. 'You think we'd tell Andy and not you? OK, you're gob almighty, everyone knows that, but no, we would never do that.'

'So are you going to tell him?' Xan asked.

'Ah shit, we'll have to, or you will, won't you? But nobody else.'

'Helen …'

'No. The more people know, the worse it's going to be. You need someone to talk to about this, so we'll have to bring Andy in, but nobody else. I know it's going to be hard, and I hate excluding her, but no, just the band. And you both have to swear not to tell a soul.' Mark sat back. 'Any arguments?'

Xan shivered. 'What if I refuse?'

'We've got a bit of money, savings. We'll take Mum and move away, change our names. She doesn't know, and I don't want her to.'

'Why not?'

'Because I suspect that our dads were like us, werewolves, whatever you want to call us. And I think that's connected to why they left. And I don't know what they told my mum and my auntie Miriam, but I know that it wasn't the truth. My mum has little enough to cling to from the past, and if she found out that my dad lied to her and I've been lying to her, she'd be devastated. She's happy now, and looking after her is the most important thing for me and John.'

Xan swallowed. 'You bastard, you know exactly how to shut me up. I can't hurt Frannie.'

John spoke up. 'Can we trust Andy?'

'Andrew Ransome? If you can get a promise out of him, he'll keep it. He's the most loyal person I've ever known. But he'll want to tell Helen. That's the hard bit.' Xan glanced at Mark. 'Are you sure your mum isn't like you?'

'Absolutely.'

'And is there anyone else? More werewolves?'

'Trust me, we've looked.' Mark bit his lip. 'Every tour, every holiday, every business trip, one or both of us went wolf and searched. Our sense of smell is different as wolves. We'd recognise the scent of another wolf, that's why we're so sure that mum isn't like us.' He shrugged. 'But we'll carry on searching, because there must be more of us. Maybe even women.'

It all became clear to Xan. 'And that's what

you're waiting for, isn't it?'

'Yeah.' Mark sighed and leaned back into the chair. 'You OK with this? Can you keep your gob shut?'

'For you, dear, anything.' Xan managed a smile. Mark nodded. It was, perhaps, going to be OK.

Xan licked his lips and leaned forwards. 'How does it happen? Can I see?'

'Fucksake,' muttered John. Mark blushed. The cousins looked at each other.

Xan shrugged. 'Sorry.'

'No, it's OK. It takes energy, though, and we've both Changed twice tonight without eating.'

'I'll cook us all a full breakfast,' Xan said soberly.

John stood and stripped, and within seconds a large, pure-black wolf stood in his place. Xan approached cautiously and looked back at Mark. 'Does he know that it's me?' he asked.

Mark nodded, and Xan held his hand out. John took it between his teeth, and bit down, just enough to bruise, not hard enough to break the skin. He let go, shivered and changed back to his human form. He got dressed quickly and stared at Xan.

'Mark reckons each Change takes two or three thousand calories. That's probably ten thousand calories I've burned in just a few hours.' He stared at Xan, who got the message and headed for the kitchen.

Andy arrived the following day, curious about the message from Xan and obviously intrigued by the presence of all three of his bandmates. The message had said, 'I worked out their secret.'

Andy walked straight into Xan's house and took the most comfortable armchair in the living room. He gave Xan a quizzical look. 'So, what is it? Are they secretly Stone Roses fans or something? Or is it Dungeons and Dragons? Or Civil War re-enactment? Please, don't tell me they're Morris Men on the quiet.' He was laughing now, and Xan ruefully realised that Andy was turning into that certain type of man who finds himself endlessly entertaining.

'Best if they tell you,' Xan said quietly. 'They're outside. I'll give them a shout.'

Andy waited, hearing low voices in the kitchen. He tapped the chair arm impatiently; the band had been together for a long time, and he didn't see how any revelation could justify this much drama. Eventually, Mark walked in and took the chair opposite Andy. John and Xan took the sofa. Mark waited quietly until he had Andy's full attention.

'We're werewolves,' he said quietly.

'Yeah, and I'm the vampire Lestat,' Andy shot back. He grinned. 'Come on, what's really going on?'

'We're werewolves,' Mark repeated. He said nothing else.

Andy looked at John, searching for the

slightest hint of a smile. Nothing. Andy was starting to feel nervous. 'As in howling at the moon and avoiding silver bullets?'

'Some howling, yeah, but nobody's tried to shoot us yet.' Mark was very calm.

'And how does … I mean, we've played outdoor gigs under a full moon and I didn't notice anything out of the ordinary.' Andy was smiling nervously now. This kind of piss-take was out of character for Mark.

'That lunar phases stuff … nope, doesn't seem to apply to us. I don't keep track of it.' Mark glanced at John, who nodded in agreement.

'And, um, John loves garlic …'

'That's vampires,' Xan chipped in.

'And there's no such thing as vampires,' John added.

Andy decided to humour them; they were clearly all in on whatever joke this was.

'So, did you get bitten at some point? That Spanish teacher in sixth form, she was a bit hairy, wasn't she? Did she get her teeth into John?'

Mark blinked slowly. 'No. It just happened, we just … changed … when we were about fourteen. And it kept happening, and then we learned to control it.' He shrugged. 'We call it Changing.'

'I wanted to call it Transmogrifying but Mark wouldn't let me,' John said.

Andy laughed. 'Brilliant. Come on, what's all this about? An idea for a concept album? I like it, really, I'm in. It could be a lot of fun. A big full moon for the stage set, some dark forest scenery, work a bit of 'Peter and the Wolf' into some of the music. Maybe one set for the concept album and a shorter set for fan favourites and greatest hits? We could wear red contact lenses and…'

Mark interrupted. 'We're werewolves.' He glanced at John, who was undressing.

Andy shook his head. 'Oh, come on, I know he's hairy but … oh fuck. Oh …' He sank back into the chair and stared. 'No. No,' he whispered.

The huge black wolf rolled on to his back and waved his legs in the air. Mark fought a grin, gave up and laughed at his cousin. Xan watched, entranced, and Andy closed his eyes. When he opened them again, John was back in human form, zipping up his jeans.

'OK, you spiked my drink and I'm hallu—'

'We're werewolves, Andy. We're human, but we can change into wolf form. Ask me a question.'

Andy stood and went to the kitchen; he came back with a glass full of whisky. He knocked half of it back and stared at Mark. 'Why didn't you tell me before?'

'Because we want this to be a secret. Because we don't know how people will react. Xan found out, last night, because he's the nosiest person on this planet, and frankly I expected him to find out ten years ago. Anyway, it's a secret, but Xan can't keep a secret from you so here we are, telling you too. And we don't want either of you to tell anyone else. Even Helen.'

'No, I can see that.' Andy blinked. 'Will I see

that again? That … Transmogrification?'

'Change,' Mark said, frowning at John, who was smirking. 'Yeah, if we can trust you.'

'Both of you can do that?'

'Yes.' Mark nodded.

Andy finished the drink. 'What else can you do? Just wolves?'

Mark blinked. 'Just?'

'Oh, you know what I mean. Do you do any other animals, can you change how you look, change sex even?' He was fascinated.

'I have no idea.' Mark looked very taken aback. He turned to John. 'Can we?'

'Never tried, never thought of trying. Come on, Andy, you can't pretend that wasn't impressive.'

Andy took a deep breath. 'I want it.'

'What?' Mark blinked.

'Whatever it takes, I want it. I want to be able to do that. What would it take? A bite?'

'I … we … I don't know. I've never even dreamed of … you want this? Why?'

'Why not?' Andy had regained his composure and was looking intently at Mark.

'Because if people find out, we don't know what they'll do. Experiments, probably. And they might hurt Mum.'

Andy nodded. 'Yeah, the thought crossed my mind, which is why I won't tell anyone, and why Xan won't tell anyone. I'll keep your secret, without any conditions. But I want you to try to infect me, because we're friends and I want to be part of this.'

'And me…' Xan said nervously.

'And him too,' Andy said. 'Come on, it'll be cool, the four of us, sharing this.' He laughed. 'Is this why you never sleep? I've always wondered…'

Mark swallowed. 'We tried to hide that.'

'You can't, not when we used to share hotel rooms or when you always volunteer to drive at night.'

Mark took a deep breath. 'We need sleep, a minimum of four hours every three days, but we can sleep a lot more, if we need to. If we're recovering from an injury, we need more than that. If we've Changed recently, we need an extra couple of hours.'

'Ah, yes, injuries. Like when John broke his wrist then the next day he was fine and tried to tell me it was just a sprain.'

'We heal fast, but not instantly,' John said. 'Although a Change always helps.'

'And we can get ill, we can catch viruses and stuff,' Mark explained, 'but if we change to wolf and back again, it seems to eliminate most things straight away. Some need a couple of Changes, but I've never had a bug I couldn't get rid of.'

'Yeah, I noticed.' Andy nodded. 'And I want that. Christ, an hour a night? I need seven, or sometimes eight, and I could do so much with those extra hours. Of course, I'd have to be quiet … Helen would notice otherwise.'

Mark sighed. 'OK, we'll try. But she'll ask about the bite. How will you explain that?'

Andy shrugged. 'I'll think of something. When do we start?'

Chapter 11

Joyce chose her moment carefully, moving up behind him as he bent to stow his gym clothes in the boot of his car. He was bigger and stronger than her, and she knew that he was just as vicious. Surprise was key, and she used every bit of her advantage. She could be very quiet. He must have seen some movement reflected in the metallic sheen of his car, because he turned as he straightened up. She kept her knives very sharp and came up from a crouch to hit his kidney and groin. He doubled over, staring at her in disbelief as she spun and opened his throat.

There was a lot of blood, but she'd chosen her moment well and tonight there would be a lot of rain, which would cleanse the scene and turn the nearby river into a torrent. She stripped the body and pocketed the cash from the wallet, putting everything else, together with the knives, into a hessian rucksack, which she shrugged on to her shoulders. She took hold of her victim's feet and dragged him to the riverbank. She waded out until she was knee deep in the shallows, swung the body around and let the current take it. If she was lucky, it would stay in the main flow and wash out to sea before the tide turned. The longer the body stayed in the water, the happier she'd be. She was good at making murder look like suicide, but this time her client wanted there to be no doubt of how her son had died.

She walked upstream for two miles until she

got to a bridge, where she crossed and strolled through housing estates until she reached a bus stop. She checked the rucksack for bloodstains and, finding none, jumped on to the next bus and rode for three stops. Another half-mile walk and she reached her own car. She was home within an hour, and headed straight for the garden incinerator, where she destroyed her victim's clothes, wallet and the cheap rucksack. She put her knives to soak in the kitchen in hot soapy water.

Diana wandered into the kitchen. 'What are you up to?'

Joyce bit her lip. 'I thought you were working late?'

Diana shrugged. 'Power cut in the lab – they sent me home. I thought I had the house to myself. The others are out clubbing. Where did those knives come from? They look sharp.'

Joyce sighed. 'They're mine, for my cookery course. If I leave 'em in the kitchen you'll use them and they'll get ruined.'

'Oh. OK. What were you burning?'

'Diana! What's with the third degree? OK, I interviewed an old lady last week about her childhood in Africa and she took a liking to me and gave me some of her old dresses. When I opened the bag earlier everything was moth-ridden. I decided to just burn the lot.'

'OK.' Joyce's younger sister smiled brightly. 'I was going to make a meal, do you fancy a fry-up? We've got eggs, steak and some kidneys. I've soaked the kidneys so they're not too pissy.'

Joyce shook her head. 'No, not tonight. I'm not hungry. Give me a minute to finish cleaning my knives and I'll get out of your way.'

'Sure.' Diana stopped at the doorway. 'How's things going with the new book? I do wish you'd reconsider the title. "*Furry Tails and Fairy Tales*" is a bit naff.'

'I'll think about it,' Joyce said calmly. She listened as Diana made her way upstairs and when she heard a door shut, she finished cleaning and drying her knives and went out to the incinerator to stir the ashes. There was a distinctive clasp from the wallet, some fragments of a zip and a pair of shoe buckles. Joyce went to the shed and grabbed a pack of brown paper bags and a plastic glove. She put the glove in her pocket, and each item in a separate bag, then left the house. She called out to Diana, 'Just going for a walk, back in an hour.'

It didn't take long to find enough dog shit on the pavements to bulk out each bag, and she dropped them into separate rubbish bins in the area. When she got back she allowed herself to relax, and by the time her other housemates were home, she was curled up in an armchair reading a novel.

The following day she placed a classified ad in five regional newspapers, asking for unusual family stories related to angels. A week later the envelopes started to arrive at her PO box. They contained cash and postal orders, and brief, unsigned, messages of thanks.

Eventually, the body washed up and was identified. A much-loved family man, the newspapers said, a popular sportsman and business leader. Even the rough print of the newspapers showed the faded bruise on the face of his widow. His acquittals on three charges of rape over the years were not even mentioned. She took cuttings and hid them carefully.

Chapter 12

'When did you last sleep?' Joyce asked her sister.

'When I was last tired,' Diana replied, peering at a knitting pattern, then at a swatch of knitting. 'What do you think of this stitch? I think maybe a smaller needle would do it more justice…'

Joyce rolled her eyes. Knitting needles could be quite useful, in the right circumstances, but using them to knit with was not something she'd ever considered. Diana had found her collection of steel needles and appropriated them. Joyce knew that all four of her housemates had a tendency to become obsessed with things, but Diana really did outshine them all. Two weeks into Diana's new hobby and all five women were already kitted out with new scarves and bobble hats. Diana was experimenting with more advanced techniques, and Joyce had given up on ever getting her needles back. She supposed that she should consider herself lucky that her younger sister hadn't suddenly taken an interest in cooking and nicked her knives too.

Joyce persisted. 'Have you been to work?'

Diana looked up. 'I'm not daft, of course I have.'

'Good, I was worried that you'd be upset…'

'That I didn't get the PhD placement? Don't worry, more letters might be fun one day, but I'm enjoying my work and I don't mind doing research assistantships. Also, if I do a PhD then I might get a more hands-on supervisor, and that's the last thing I want.'

Joyce nodded. Diana was doing some private research after hours and she said that having access to the genetics labs was as important as having paid work.

'OK.' Joyce started to walk away, and Diana spoke up.

'Joyce, you don't have to do this, you know? The whole housemother thing? I'm twenty-eight now and the others are all over thirty. I mean, I know it's good for us all to help each other, but we don't have to always be together, do we?'

'Am I that overbearing?' Joyce asked, frowning.

'Over-protective, maybe.' Diana shrugged. 'You did something amazing, tracking down Lorraine and Cynth and Trisha, and it's been fun, living together, but sometimes I get the feeling that they might want to move on, get their own places.' She bit her lip. 'They won't say anything to you, they think they owe you for bringing everyone together and showing them that they're not alone. I think you should maybe start dropping hints that we can be a group without living in each other's pockets.'

'Living in your house, you mean?' Joyce frowned.

'No, it's not like that. And don't take that tone, I don't mean you, and you know that the house is mine because that's what you wanted. You wanted me to have the security of my own place in case anything happened to you, remember?'

Joyce remembered. Even though Diana thought that her sister lived a quiet, academic life,

Joyce knew that if a job went wrong she could die or end up in prison. She'd made sure that the house they'd bought together was in Diana's name. It wasn't as if Joyce didn't have money piling up in various accounts; she had a knack for making money, and no impulse to spend any of it.

'We're safer together,' Joyce said.

'Yeah, you say that, but we're actually less visible as wolves if we run singly or in pairs. Don't get me wrong, I like living with you all, but the others uprooted their lives to join us here, and sometimes I get the impression that they'd like a bit more autonomy.' Diana shrugged. 'Just a thought.'

Joyce turned away and went to her room, where she lay on her bed and shook her head. 'Just a thought,' she muttered. 'Twenty years of looking after her, and now she's having thoughts.' She took a deep breath. Maybe Diana's claims to be a capable adult held some truth, and maybe it was time for Joyce to break free. Maybe even time to do what Diana had no interest in doing. Perhaps she ought to look for more Shifters, and hope that this time she would find that most elusive creature, a male Shifter.

Joyce kept busy; she'd left academia years ago, but her textbooks on folklore and ethnology were required reading for several degree courses, and she was beginning to get consultancy work from TV and film companies. The travel was great cover for what she considered her second, bloodier job. She prided herself on her research and it was unthinkable that she should kill an innocent, or even someone capable of remorse, but she'd found that the majority of the requests that made their way to her were, in her opinion, reasonable.

Her first kill, her own uncle, had been a clumsy one. He'd raped her for years, in the guise of a helpful babysitter, but he'd left her alone after she reached puberty. Her anger had taken her out on long night-time walks, which was when she'd first Shifted, becoming a wolf when running away in terror from three drunks who'd almost caught her in a quiet park in the early hours of a summer night. She'd accepted her first change eagerly; the dark joy and feeling of utter power was a much-deserved payback for the suffering she'd experienced at her uncle's hands. Her life had changed so much in that one night, and she'd devoted herself to finding out more about werewolves. She'd taken to selling her body, careless of danger, extracting a sense of power from the need that the men revealed to her. One night she'd returned to find her uncle molesting Diana. He'd been dead within seconds, and in her rage she'd dragged his torn body around the house, leaving blood and rented flesh and bone in scattered piles. When her parents had come home, they'd found her naked and bloody in the midst of the glorious mess that had once been Uncle Steve. Diana had been sitting primly on the sofa, sipping at a glass of milk. Joyce sometimes wondered if her mother would have been more accepting of the werewolf trait if she'd found out about it in a less traumatic manner.

Her parents had covered up well; they were

both science teachers and knew how to rig a gas explosion to hide Steve's true cause of death. Diana had explained what had happened, enraging their dad enough that he'd smashed what was left of his brother's head into an unrecognisable mess. The insurance had paid out, and they'd all moved away from the London suburb and back to their old home town in the North East. Joyce had given up her evening activities in favour of intense study of folklore and languages: she was going to find out what she was and where she'd come from. Her parents, clearly, were not werewolves.

And then Diana had Shifted too, and Joyce found that her feelings towards her sister had become almost obsessively protective. She hated leaving her young sister behind when it was time to go to university. When Dad died, far too young, and Mum had lashed out at the girls in her grief, Joyce had taken Diana away and pulled strings to make sure that her younger sister got a place at the University of Manchester where Joyce was already working. That had been ten years ago and maybe, just maybe, it was time for Joyce to take a deep breath and let Diana make her own way in the world.

She spent the next few days on a trip to Aberdeen, where she was interviewing locals for their tales of witches and fey folk. Her grasp of Doric and Scots Gaelic was a little rusty, but good enough to convince people of her respect for their stories and traditions. She collected a dozen stories, most of them were variants on other Scots stories, but two were new to her. She arrived home happy and excited, and rushed into her room to start work.

Diana knocked on the door. It was a brief knock, the kind that was less of a request and more of a declaration; the door flew open and she strode in. Joyce sighed when she saw that her younger sister was deathly pale, her red hair a tumbled cloud.

'What's up now?' Joyce asked.

Diana threw a thick folder on to the bed.

Joyce swallowed hard. 'Where did you find this?' she demanded.

'That's not the point. Why do you have a file on murdered men? A file of men murdered when you weren't at home. A file of unsolved murders. And what makes me really suspicious, a file of murdered killers and rapists. This … this is…' Diana shook her head. 'Why?'

Joyce took a deep breath. 'Why? Because nobody else would do it. Because the police won't listen and the CPS won't prosecute and the courts won't convict. Someone has to act.'

Diana sighed. 'I don't mean why kill them, you idiot. I mean, why keep a bloody file? Anyone could have found it. Look, you've been clever – different causes of death, different locations, some of them aren't even suspicious deaths, according to the obituaries. I'm not saying I approve, but I'm not going to turn you in, am I? I just … I don't want you doing this and living with me. I'm sorry, Joyce, I've got some really interesting work going on in the lab, and I can't afford to get mixed up in your … hobby.'

Joyce glared at her younger sister, unused to being on the back foot.

'It's not just a hobby, I get paid. There's a system, word of mouth…'

Diana stared, open-mouthed. 'People know about this? You bloody idiot. I mean, random murders are one thing, but running a business … I don't believe it. How do people contact you, pay you? No, don't tell me, I don't want to know. I really do not want to know. Bloody hell, Joyce, I knew you had issues but I didn't think you'd actually kill again.'

Joyce snarled. 'Again. That's the point, isn't it? *Again.* Because that first kill, that was to protect you, and everything I've done since then has been to protect you.'

Diana held up a photo of a sixty-year-old man, killed on the road when the brakes on his bike failed. 'This guy was no threat to me.' She said quietly.

'OK, not just you. Women, girls. Even young lads. You know what I mean. Someone has to do it.'

'I can't let that someone be you. Joyce, how can you heal if you carry on killing? I know you have demons.'

'I am the demon,' Joyce growled.

'Yeah, sure you are.' Diana rolled her eyes. 'You're a middle-class folklorist and academic, Joyce, you're my big sister and…'

Joyce grabbed the file. 'Don't you dare tell me what I am. I've spent my life protecting you, guiding you…'

'Did I ask you to?' Diana said calmly. 'I don't think I ever did. I think I'd like you to leave. And I'm going to burn these cuttings.'

'I'll burn them,' Joyce said quietly. 'You're right, it was stupid to keep them.'

Diana left the file on the bed, nodded and walked out.

The next day Joyce was gone, leaving no explanation, just her literary agent's phone number. Within days the other Shifters were making plans to leave, unnerved by Joyce's disappearance and Diana's foul mood. Within a week, Diana was alone in the house. With the other women gone she had time on her hands. She started in the attics and worked down, cleaning away evidence of her former housemates. She could still smell them when she took her wolf form in the dead of night; there were traces of them in the garden, on the walls and in the dirt. It was unbearable, and she scrubbed the walls with alcohol and detergents, and dug the soil until the smell was gone. Eventually, the house was her own, and she told herself that she was happy, that she was fulfilled by her work and that she didn't need the company of werewolves.

Chapter 13

Xan opened his eyes slowly and smiled appreciatively at the woman who was straddling him. Her eyes were still half lidded, and she groaned and fell backwards on to the bed.

He cuddled up, he loved to cuddle. She seemed surprised but let him.

'Jen, I hope you're not busy tomorrow,' he whispered. 'I'd like you to stay tonight.'

She lay still. 'What do you want to do tomorrow?' she asked cautiously.

Ah, tread carefully, Xan. 'Um, I'm busy with the guys. I can't really spend time with you. I just think it would be nice to spend the night together. I mean, I'll drive you home, after breakfast…'

'Just get me to a train station. Do you want my number?'

Years ago, he would have said yes, he would have reasoned that she knew the game as well as he did. Those bastard Prestons had changed things, forced him to behave with more honesty.

'I'm sorry, I probably wouldn't ever use it. I don't really do long-term relationships.'

'Ah.'

He snuggled up, applying XanSense. 'That doesn't mean I don't do relationships, y'know? It's just that they're very short, very intense and as close to perfect as I can get them.'

She laughed. 'Just don't send flowers, OK?'

'If that's how you want it.' His hand stole up to caress her breast. 'Do you mind if I put the video on?'

'Uh?'

'Your video … I taped it off the telly last week, I collect good videos.' He lay on his belly and looked at her. She was sitting up now and it was a fine view. 'And it is a good video, lots of nice references. Did you have much input? We had fuck-all chance to comment on our first four vids – luckily they all turned out half decent.'

She was more relaxed now, flattered. 'You really watched my vid?'

'Yup. Sexy girl, great song, stupendous percussion…'

'That's my sister…'

'I know.' Xan grinned. 'I know all. I'm a fan.'

'Damn groupies,' Jen teased.

The door downstairs slammed and they both jumped. Heavy footsteps on the stairs, and Xan rolled his eyes. 'He'll just storm in,' he warned her, and she slid down the bed and covered herself just before the door flew open and a powerfully built man launched himself on to the bed, noticing at the last minute that it was doubly occupied and twisting to land in an awkward crouch at its foot.

'Whoops, oh, hiya, Jen. Fancy seeing you here.' He grinned, getting off the bed and sitting on the window ledge. 'Did I interrupt anything?'

Xan scowled. 'You know each other?'

'Yeah, course we do.' The newcomer flashed a big grin at the young woman. 'Remember me? John Preston?'

'Oh…' she blushed. 'So it was you. I wasn't

sure.'

'Yeah, the excitement of the wedding day, I 'spect.' John winked at her.

'This sounds juicy: tell all.' Xan had recovered now, and Jen winced.

'It was my hen night, I was very drunk. I got chatted up…'

'Oh John!' Xan sounded genuinely reproachful, which earned him a cynical look from both John and Jen.

'I got chatted up and followed the guy out of the club. I knew I was being stupid, but I wasn't sure if it was the infidelity or the marriage itself that I was unsure of. I didn't realise until I was halfway into the car and being pushed the rest of the way in that there were two other guys in the car.'

'John?' Xan was confused.

'Let her tell the story.' John crossed his legs, looking embarrassed now.

'Next thing I know, I'm not being pushed, I'm being pulled out of the car, the guy who'd been pushing me was flat on his arse in a puddle, and some guy has a firm grip on me and I'm about to scream, when I get the message that he's asking me if I really wanted to get in the car and would I like to get some water and sober up a bit.' She glanced at John. 'He stayed with me, walked me around town until I was sober and made sure that I got home safely. And he sent flowers and best wishes for the wedding.'

'I assume the marriage didn't work out?' John asked.

'Nope.' She shrugged. 'At least I got it over with young, and decided to start having fun. Big sis got divorced same month as me, we decided to say a big fuck-off to our exes and start a band. Next thing we've been signed up to a label and we're gigging. You guys didn't really make it big for another few years after the hen night. When I saw you on telly, I thought you looked like my white knight, but I didn't really think it could have been you. Thank you.'

'You're welcome. I just wish I could have decked the other two creeps.'

'I'm just surprised that you recognised me so quickly.'

John shrugged. 'Truth is, Xan's a big fan of yours. He kept playing the video and nagging me about it. It kinda dawned on me that I'd seen you before, but I couldn't quite put my finger on it.'

'That's a first,' Xan commented darkly. He was ignored.

'I've been puzzling over it for weeks, I reckon seeing you all dishevelled made things click into place. Xan, shame on you for dishevelling the lady.'

'She made me do it.' Xan grinned. 'Anyway, you know, fuck off.'

John nodded. 'Sorry. Oh, can I stay over tonight? Manchester is horrible and I need fresh air.'

Xan understood. 'It's a bit too fresh for me. I'll have the windows closed and the curtains drawn, and Jen and I are planning a lie-in.'

John nodded, a flash of gratitude in his eyes.

'Jen, make sure you leave your number for me, maybe we could go for a drink sometime?'

He left the room and the door slammed behind him.

'Well, someone wants my number,' Jen said eventually.

Xan sighed. 'Yeah, John, he'll call you back, he'll see you again, he'll send you a card on significant birthdays, he'll be utterly sweet, but never think he's yours. He's not made for settling down.'

'And you?' Now all that was out of the way, things were more relaxed.

'Me? I'm settled down. This is it!' Xan waved his hand, indicating the spacious, modern bedroom. 'This is home, this is where I'll stay.' He paused for effect. 'One day, if I'm feeling like getting domesticated, I may get a cat, a big tomcat that pees on the walls and digs up the flower beds. I will retire from my wild existence and devote myself to his welfare, and write sonnets in his honour while acquiring a distinct odour of cat piss myself. People will carefully stand several yards from me when I do business with them, and I will woefully neglect my personal grooming. But that, my friend, is for the future. For now, you find yourself in the company of Xan Kendrick, rock star supreme, drummer, lover, darling favourite of a thousand music journos. And I don't smell of cat pee.'

'For which I am truly thankful.' Jen laughed, cuddling up to him again. 'I wish I was that big tomcat, though.'

'Honey, you ain't got the balls for it,' he

assured her, reaching for the condoms.

Xan woke first, grabbing his short red bathrobe from the back of the bedroom door and wandering downstairs to make breakfast. He could already smell coffee, and hot fat. As he was halfway to the kitchen the sizzle and aroma of frying bacon made him grin widely.

The open plan stairs led into the living room, where John lay on the sofa reading a newspaper.

'Who's cooking?' Xan yawned.

'Your wife,' John said and returned to his perusal of the crossword puzzle.

Xan stuck his tongue out at his bandmate and cowered in mock fear as John roared, 'I saw that.'

He pushed the kitchen door open and peered in. 'Hey, Andy,' he said gently.

'Hey yourself,' Andy replied, putting down the butter knife. 'Gimme a hug.'

The hug became a kiss, and the kiss deepened until Xan drew away, breathless. 'I thought you and Helen were away.'

Andy returned to his sandwich-making. 'Yeah, got back early hours. She's still in bed but I got restless, decided to drive up to see you. She'll be along for lunch, she said, she needs more sleep than I do.'

Xan understood; Helen needed more sleep than Andy since the Prestons had successfully infected him with whatever made them into something … something else. Helen was lucky not to know what was going on, and didn't have to suffer the excruciating jealousy that wore away at Xan's heart. The attempts to infect Xan hadn't worked. Jen had commented on the twisted scars, and he'd brushed aside her concern with a comment about dangerous sports.

Andy was looking at him expectantly. 'How many for breakfast then? John told me you had company…'

The question went unsaid. *Have we lost you?* Andy meant.

Xan smiled, making it as filthy as he could. 'Jen Conway, singer with Oaf Uckitt. She'll be having breakfast with us. She's cool. I met her yesterday when I was in London doing promo stuff, we're label mates. We set up a mutual admiration society in the corridor, and here we are.'

'Marriage? Babies? Labrador puppies?' Andy arched an eyebrow.

'Breakfast, final round in bed, lift to the station and "I will never forget you".' Xan shrugged. 'What can I say? My heart is already taken.'

Andy kissed him again. 'I hope you're talking about me, and not that skinny wretch Mark Preston.'

'Ah, you see, you and Helen got married, and you meant it. If I'd married Hel, it would have been a bit of a piss-take. You did it, and everyone believes it.'

'She didn't want a piss-take,' Andy said quietly.

'I know. I know that.' Xan shook his fine

blond hair out of his eyes. 'I'll go and tell Jen that breakfast is nearly ready. I'll set the table for four.'

'Five. Mark arrived just before I did, but he's gone for a long walk. You know, that kind of long walk with his hands buried in his pockets as he strides, head down, across the moor.'

'What's up with him now?'

'Blue balls, I reckon. I know he's made his stupid vow of celibacy, but he doesn't have to make life miserable for the rest of us. He gets moodier every fucking week, and he wasn't a ray of sunshine on day one.' Andy finished making the first sandwich and stuck it in the oven to keep it warm. 'He'll be back soon; he can smell bacon from ten miles away.'

They exchanged a wry look that said it all. Yeah, we love him, but he's a pain in the arse.

Xan made his way back upstairs and asked Jen if she wanted to eat with the guys or if she'd rather share breakfast in bed with him.

She grabbed her overnight bag and sashayed into the bathroom, clearly inviting him to join her, but he realised he'd never get out if he played that game. He went back downstairs and set the table: a domestic ritual that made him happy. He loved the way that his friends just dropped by and made his house their second home.

Mark came in, all smiles, just as Jen came downstairs, and seemed to be genuinely interested to meet her. To Xan's surprise, he monopolised the young woman throughout the meal, and looked disappointed when Xan stepped in to ask Jen to join him upstairs to 'sort out that thing we were talking about'.

He took her to the station and waited for her train to leave before he drove home. He got back to the house and found the rest of the band in the practice room at the back. He wasn't surprised; this was how it worked. Andy had been on holiday with Helen, so they'd been apart for a few weeks, and now it was time to get back together and see what they could create. Xan had no doubt that whatever came from the four of them would be very, very good.

Mark and Andy were having a half-hearted argument about Mark's claim that Andy's bass was out of tune. Of course, if Mark said it was, then it was, and Andy was just arguing for the fun of it, to pass the time until Xan took his place on his drum stool and picked up his sticks.

Ba Dum CRASH. The drums spoke, the cymbals cried for attention, and the bass player and guitarist stopped squabbling and turned to Xan, all smiles.

Xan gave a tiny bow. 'I hereby call all present to witness the flirtation, foreplay and downright dirty fucking around that will lead to the conception, gestation and delivery of the best bloody rock album this planet has ever seen. Let's get it on, my darlings.'

John nodded and switched on the recording gear; his role at this stage was chief critic. Later he'd develop a vocal line, or perhaps wait until Xan gave him some lyrics to wrap his voice around. For now, he was their tech, roadie, tea-maker and audience.

'Andrew Ransome, tune that fucking bass,' Mark said.

'You do it,' Andy said, mock humble, and Mark rolled his eyes and took the instrument.

They'd learned to each take their turn; they all had ideas for new songs and they knew by now that there was time enough for everyone to air their ideas and get the attention they deserved. They played around for an hour or so, then returned to an old hit, one of John's favourites, to give him a chance to stretch his vocal cords a bit. They were just riffing their way around the end of the song, having fun, when the door opened and a tall, elegant blonde woman slipped inside the room, taking a seat against the far wall. They all nodded to her and carried on, gradually calming down. Mark finished with a superb, showy, sarcastic guitar-god solo, and Xan laid his sticks down carefully.

Helen sat with her arms crossed. 'So you guys aren't splitting up, after all?' Nobody spoke; they were all still happily breathless. 'Well, if you can't be bothered talking to me…' she said, laughing, her eyes on Xan, '…I'll go back home.'

Andy reached her first, hugging her briefly before leaving the room. Mark and John made their excuses and followed Ransome.

Xan stood up. 'Three weeks, and not a postcard in sight.'

'We rang you three times a week!' Helen protested. But she was smiling. 'Quit winding me up, Kendrick. I've missed you.'

'Yeah? Well, same goes.'

'Who was the woman?' Helen asked casually.

Xan narrowed his eyes and studied his fingernails. 'Andy arrived earlier, brought some tramp with him, said he needed a change…'

Helen's laughter peeled around the room. 'You lying dog. There's a pay-and-display ticket on your dashboard for the station car park, this morning. There's lipstick on a coffee cup in the kitchen, five dirty plates from breakfast, and there are four used condoms in your bedroom waste bin.'

'Three' – Xan licked his lips – 'Miss Marple.'

'OK, that last was a guess.' She wrinkled her nose. 'So, who was she?'

'She's called Jen Conway.'

Helen yelled in triumph. 'Yes! I win!'

'What-the-fuck-Helen-make-sense-will-ya?' Xan drawled, a mantra almost as old as speech to him.

'I saw her vid on TV when we were in Austria. Andy said she was on the same label as you. I said that you'd bed her before the year was out. He said that John would get there first. He owes me a week's housework. Fan-bloody-tastic.'

'There have been others,' Xan said, mustering his dignity.

'Yeah, I know, babe. Come here.'

He narrowed his eyes again. 'I don't just come running, you know?'

'Xan, I want a hug,' she said, her voice a little quieter now, and he couldn't resist her – not when she used that voice.

They sat on the floor together, her arm around him, his head nestled to her breast. Xan reflected that his claim to be free of sexual jealousy had a limit: Helen was his, and Andy's, and if she ever left them he'd die of misery. He gave a sad little sigh, signalling that he'd been sorely neglected and wanted some attention.

'What's up, beautiful?' Helen asked quietly.

'I've got such a stupid crush on him. It's been, what, twelve years now? You'd think I'd get over it.'

'You do, regularly.' She held him closer.

'Yeah, but then he looks at me with those big brown eyes, or he flicks his hair back, or asks me to show him a new technique on the drums, or … Helen, he's the only one I've ever really wanted.'

'Charming,' she said, unperturbed.

'I'm not counting you and Andy, you daft bint,' he whispered. 'Why am I so obsessed?'

'Because he's always around, and he's not interested in you, not in that way.'

'He's not interested in me at all,' Xan whined.

'Baby, he's fascinated by you, he loves you to bits, but he's straight as hell, and even if he wasn't, he's wise enough to know that it would be a disaster – it would pull the band apart.'

'He's a virgin, he can't possibly know if he's straight or not.'

'Well, he does,' Helen said firmly. 'Andy leaves him alone, and I wish you would too.'

'But I want him,' Xan said, pouting.

'Tough shit.' Helen stood up. 'Xan, I was bored with this conversation ten years ago, and it's not getting any more interesting as we get older.'

'Helen, why can't I settle down with some nice lass and live happily ever after?'

Helen had no answer, just a sympathetic smile.

Xan stood too, and adopted a dark look. 'You didn't see Mark with Jen, he was having a major conversation with her. He looked really pissed off when I interrupted them.'

'What were they talking about?' Helen asked casually.

'Oh, I dunno. Something about guitars…'

'Yeah? Xan, she's a guitarist, and a good one. He was talking to a fellow musician. Come on, lad, let's get some lunch. You look half starved, has nobody been looking after you?'

Chapter 14

Sometimes Mark wondered if he should find a place of his own. Granted, he'd bought his mum a bigger house when he hit the money, but he hadn't moved out. It suited him there, and he was always welcome at Xan's.

He was currently hanging around at Xan's. The house backed on to a small lake, and it felt so good to walk naked across the back lawn and into the cold black water, letting his legs go almost numb before he started to swim across to the other side. Ten laps before breakfast, then he'd stumble back across the lawn, his skin blue and his balls hauled so high he almost lost them. Xan would usually still be in bed, music blaring out from his room.

Xan had asked him to move in, more than once, but Mark liked his independence, and had a mild suspicion that Xan's intentions towards him had a carnal aspect that didn't suit him one bit. Hanging around and repaying Xan's hospitality by cooking and keeping the place tidy did suit him, though, and he noticed with mild pleasure that the skinny man usually gained a few pounds whenever he stayed over.

Mid morning and Andy turned up, a great grey wolf staring in through the patio windows. How far had he come like that, unashamedly furry? It was still all new for him, and he loved to be a wolf whenever they were in private together. Mark opened the door and Andy sniffed around, licked his hand, and loped upstairs.

Mark made his way to Xan's rehearsal room and cleared away the sweet wrappers and pop cans from around the drums. Finally, satisfied that all was clean, he changed the height of the stool and the pedals and settled down to practise. Xan wasn't the best drummer he'd ever met, but he was the best he'd been privileged enough to learn from, and Mark's interest spurred his drummer on to greater things, always trying to stay two or three steps ahead of Mark's incessant thirst for skill, knowledge, technique.

Mark's wrists were aching and his teeth itching by the time he was brought out of his reverie by an impatient hand on his shoulder.

'Move over, wolf boy.' Xan removed Mark's earplug and whispered into his ear. 'I want my toy back.' Mark felt the flicker of Xan's tongue at his earlobe and turned to stare at his friend. Xan blushed and backed away.

The guitarist shrugged; this wasn't something he was prepared to discuss. Xan and Andy hadn't made any secret of their bisexuality and their desire for him, or for John, for that matter. John had cheerfully told them right from the start, that if they mithered him, he'd thump them. They'd taken it well, teasing John that a tussle might be just the thing to get him to let his hair down. Mark had explained, just once, that it was a non-issue, he wasn't going to be distracted by sex until he'd found the right woman. Xan's eyes had twinkled.

'For a virgin, you're pretty sure that you're straight,' he'd said, gently mocking.

'Yeah, I am,' Mark had said, with a distant smile, picking up his guitar and changing the subject.

Mark settled down on a battered old sofa to watch Xan limber up on the drums, reflecting that Xan's interest was about as flattering as having your leg humped by a randy puppy. But his friendship was much more important to Mark; it wasn't something that was offered freely or often, and Mark treasured it.

Xan had limbered up and was going through his exercises. It took a lot of practice and discipline to build up the skills necessary to appear so shambolic on stage. Mark realised that Xan was eyeing him impatiently, needing an audience. Mark nodded attentively and watched as Xan threw a stick into the air. He made a complete cock-up of it and the stick fell behind his shoulder, spinning unpredictably. Xan winked, reached behind his back, collected it smoothly and carried on drumming. Mark laughed and Xan stopped.

'You won't be able to do that unless nobody can see behind you,' he said. 'Nice sleight of hand, though.'

Xan grinned. 'I knew you'd think that. It's not a spare stick, I really caught it. Get behind me, I'll do it again.'

He repeated the trick, and Mark whistled his appreciation. 'Very, very good. But keep a spare stick behind you just in case…'

'You fuckin' bet I will.'

It was pure pleasure to watch his bandmates

practise, innovate, search for themes and explore them. Xan's place was the ideal venue for that; it was private and secluded, and nobody complained about the noise. Mark closed his eyes, lost in the complex patterns that Xan was weaving. The promise of a melody danced just beyond his grasp and he nodded – it would come when he needed it. Meanwhile, something else was happening, Andy was tuning up his bass, and joining Xan, the Ransomed Hearts rhythm section trying out new combinations. Mark felt that familiar restlessness taking over again, and reached for a guitar. He tuned it meticulously, staring at Andy's bass and nodding. Andy looked relieved.

Mark stayed seated, almost reclining, caressing the strings for a while before reaching into the pleccie pocket of his denims and starting to search for that teasing melody. Something was happening now and he vaguely wondered if anyone would have the good sense to switch on the tape recorder to preserve the ideas.

The studio door slammed open, heralding John's arrival.

John leaned against a wall, humming gently, finding a vocal line and making nonsense noises to fill it. It wasn't how the song would develop, Mark knew that instinctively, and John would realise it too. Mark threw him a hint, realising that the rhythm section had stopped and were listening to him. John nodded and abandoned his first try. The second was better and the third was right.

'We have an embryo,' Xan announced

gravely, and they all looked at each other. The thrill of a new song, coming from nowhere, never waned.

Chapter 15

The band made arrangements to spend Sunday to Friday, nine to seven, working together. There was room for flexibility – there always was – and Mark was nominated to go over to Yorkshire to grab a quick meeting with the rep from the record label, who was in the area for the weekend.

He came back on Tuesday, looking very subdued. Xan noticed that there was a difference in him and took him aside.

'What's up? You've been gone for days, we were getting worried.'

'Oh, I stayed in Leeds for a while, then I went to see Mum.'

Xan felt a stab of jealousy, Mark and Frances were close, and Xan would have loved to have that kind of relationship. That said, why was Mark moody after spending time with his mother?

'Is Auntie Fran OK?' Xan asked. He'd claimed Frances as 'Auntie' within minutes of meeting her. She didn't know quite what to make of him and had settled on an attitude of disapproving affection.

'Mum's fine.' Mark managed a smile. 'How's things going here? Have you missed me?'

'Nope, not a bit. We've decided that we don't need a guitarist and you're fired.' Xan was hurt; Mark was supposed to be his friend, and wasn't confiding in him.

Mark ignored the joke. ''K, I'll go and join the others. Is Hel around? I need a bit of privacy tonight.'

Xan swallowed the hurt; it was Mark's way of saying that he needed to change, to run, to do something that excluded Xan.

'Helen and Andy are having a quiet night in together tonight. Andy's leaving here at seven. Does that fit into your plans?'

Mark nodded, oblivious. 'Sure. I need to talk to John.'

He walked away and Xan stood watching him. What was it about this guy that was so beguiling? And once again, Xan was being left out. He followed Mark to the music room but too late to find out what he'd said to John, who'd stopped what he was doing and was following Mark back out.

Andy met Xan's glare and shrugged. Sometimes the cousins needed time together, just as Andy and Xan did.

The Prestons came back half an hour later, John looking uncharacteristically serious and Mark somewhat relieved.

'We need to talk to both of you,' Mark said quietly. 'This isn't band business.'

'Wolf business? Shall I go?' Xan asked. He'd tried to keep his voice level, and winced at the sarcastic tone that he'd actually used.

Mark glanced at Xan. 'Wolf business, but I don't keep anything from you. I thought that was understood. I had to talk to John first, that's all.'

'Spill,' Andy said.

Mark bit his lip. 'I've met a woman.'

'Wolf?' Andy asked, very quickly – too

quickly for Xan's liking.

'No, that's the point. I'm twenty-nine next month, and I'm going to stop looking. We'll carry on running together, it's safest that way, for all of us, but I can't spend the rest of my life like this – I need a home of my own. I spoke to John because if I can persuade this lass that I'm good enough for her, he'll be the only one left single, so if we do find a wolfie woman, he'll be the obvious candidate for her.'

'I always was.' John smirked. 'Nothing's changed.'

'Everything has changed,' Mark said. 'I want you to meet her, soon.'

'Tell us all about her,' Andy said, after a period of uncomfortable quiet. This announcement was unexpected and unsettling.

Mark nodded, and drew out a strip of photo booth pictures. Xan rolled his eyes.

'Damn you, Mark, do you have to be such a fucking walking cliché?'

'Apparently, yes.' Mark said, unbothered, passing the photos around. It wasn't as bad as Xan had feared; only the woman was on the pictures, so there were no smoochy snaps to endure. He stared at the image, wondering why the paper didn't burst into flames. The woman appeared to be a little self-conscious, was looking away from the camera, and there was a flush to her cheeks that Xan had to admit was quite appealing. Her straight black hair was cut in a short, expensive-looking layered bob, and she had dark eyes – not as attractive as Mark's, but still pretty. Her skin colour almost matched John's, with a hint of olive. Her features were regular and attractive, and Xan saw that she could probably be beautiful, in the right light, with the right expression on her face.

'Cute,' he said dismissively. 'Barmaid? Shop assistant?'

'Surgeon,' Mark said, sounding vaguely shocked. 'She's a surgeon. She's so dedicated and so brainy. You wouldn't think she'd look at me twice, would you?'

Xan swallowed and looked away, and was surprised when he was drawn into a bear hug by John.

'It was never gonna be you anyway,' John said, so quietly that only Xan could hear. It was true, but it didn't make it hurt any less.

Xan found his voice. 'So, have you and this wonderful woman fucked yet?'

Mark raised his eyes and fixed on Xan. 'We've had dinner together twice. As I said, I think she's the one; she's everything I ever wanted. Except for the wolfiness, obviously. I decided that I couldn't reasonably expect things to go further unless I had John's agreement that I could give up looking for a wolf woman.'

'We'll still run together?' John asked hastily.

'Yes, of course we will. Andy manages to get away from Helen, and I'll do the same. I don't like the idea of lying to my wife, but there's no other option. I can't ask Andy to lie to Helen and then expect you guys to let me share our secret with

Katie.'

'Katie,' Xan repeated. 'Wife? Mark, you don't have to marry her. Are you mad? Nobody marries their first fuck.'

Andy glanced at him, about to comment, but evidently decided to stay quiet.

'If she's the one, then I want to,' Mark said evenly.

The other three men looked at each other and decided not to argue. Mark's ethical code was a little bizarre but it didn't hurt anyone.

'Has she met Auntie Fran yet?' John asked.

'Nope. I want her to meet you lot first, I don't want to get Mum all excited if you guys are gonna scare her off.' Mark looked entirely serious when he said that, but Xan laughed, and Andy grinned.

'We'll behave ourselves,' Andy promised. 'Now, tell us how you met this paragon of womanhood.'

Mark closed his eyes for a moment, bringing his memories back.

'I met up with the guys from the label on Friday night. They want a meeting to talk money next week – Andy?'

'I'll do it,' Andy said. He was descended from a long line of successful businessmen and handled things when money was involved. 'Go on.'

'They wanted to go clubbing, some VIP place in the middle of Leeds, soccer players, soap stars, models, you know?'

'Chickadees,' John and Xan said

simultaneously.

'Yeah, that one.' Mark shrugged. 'Anyway, I got dragged into it, so I booked into a hotel. I couldn't be arsed not drinking, and wasn't sure if I'd get the privacy to Change and sober up. Anyway, I had the usual boring time in the club.'

'Hid in the cloakroom with the attendant's crossword book?' Andy asked casually.

'Not this time, the music was tolerable.' Mark smiled. 'I finally managed to escape, slept a couple of hours at the hotel, got up, nice crisp day, had breakfast and decided to find the park and go for a walk.'

'Get on with it,' John said cheerfully.

Mark shrugged. 'Well, I walked around the park a couple of times, blew the cobwebs away and sat down to watch the squirrels for a while. Mad bastards. I noticed that the lass on the bench opposite me was reading a book on fractal art, and I was trying to read the title to see if it was one I already had or not. She had it at a funny angle so I was peering at it for a while, then I realised that she thought I was looking at her and that I was making her uncomfortable.'

'She was five seconds away from hitting you with the book and running away?' Andy smirked.

'Three, probably.' Mark smiled, already nostalgic. 'So I told her that I was looking at the book, not her, and that must have pissed her off. I mean, she was mad at me when she thought I was looking at her, then mad at me again when I said I wasn't.'

'Women. Don't even try to understand them,' Andy said. John just grinned.

Mark continued. 'Next thing I know, I'm getting an exam in fractal art – she was checking that I wasn't lying. I passed the test, but I was a bit taken aback. Then I realised that I was dressed like a teenage refugee from 1980, and she was dressed really nicely, everything looked … well … classy, I suppose. Like Helen dresses, when she's got a meeting to go to. I said I was sorry if I'd made her feel anxious, and got up to go. Then she said she was sorry for making me feel bad, and told me I didn't need to go. Then she got very embarrassed and said that she thought I'd been about to try to sell her some gear, 'cept she didn't say that, she said "illegal recreational drugs". I told her that wasn't my scene, and she apologised again. She's got a really nice voice, a sort of posh North Yorkshire accent, very clear. Then she said that she was getting cold, and was going to spend the rest of the morning hanging around in a coffee shop that she knew. It took me about ten seconds to twig that she was suggesting I come with her.'

'At which point you usually run away screaming,' John observed.

'Yeah, well. Thing is, I've been doing a lot of thinking the last few weeks, since Christmas really, and I can't spend my life like this. I hate being single, and I hate people thinking that I'm weird. I just don't want to hurt anyone, you know? Then I met Katie, and I can't imagine ever hurting her. She's everything you could ever dream of: smart, funny, kind, beautiful, classy.'

'That word again.' Andy laughed. 'If I'd known you wanted a posh bird, I'd have looked up some of the girls from my old school for you.'

Mark narrowed his eyes and Andy sighed. 'Carry on, maestro,' he said.

Mark smiled. 'So, I didn't run away screaming, partly because I was interested in talking to her a bit more, partly because I was quite flattered by the attention. She had no idea that I was in a band – she still doesn't, by the way – and I must have looked a bit rough, but once we got talking, she seemed to forget how I was dressed and accept me for me, the way I spoke to her, the things we talked about.'

Xan interrupted. 'She doesn't know you're a Heart?'

'Nope, and she won't until after she's met you guys. She doesn't have the first clue about rock music. I want to know how she treats my friends, not how she acts with the Ransomed Hearts, OK?'

Xan understood. 'Sure, I'll be good,' he said, though each word tore through him. He forced himself to ask, 'So, what happened then?'

Mark smiled. 'She said she had to go home, that she had things to do. I got my nerve up and asked for her phone number. We swapped, and she noticed that mine wasn't local. She asked me where I lived, I told her and she seemed a bit put off, but then I went completely barmy and said I was staying in Leeds for a couple more days, and asked her out to dinner on Sunday.' He licked his lips, unconsciously. 'I made a few calls, worked out the kind of restaurant that would catch her attention, and scoped them out. I found one where you'd go to talk, rather than be talked about, and managed to get a table. I bought some new clothes, reserved my room for another few nights, and on Sunday night we had a really nice meal. She found out a bit more about me. I told her that I'm a musician, and she worked out that I wasn't short of a quid or two. I know it sounds awful, but I think that was important to her – she's a pretty successful lass, and she's got to be wary of guys who'll leech off her. I dropped her off at her place, a nice flat in town, and asked if she'd go to dinner again.'

John was wide-eyed. 'You didn't even kiss her?'

'I barely know her,' Mark said. 'I want to take this step by step.'

'Wazzock,' muttered Xan.

'Anyway,' Mark continued, 'we went out again last night to see a film, then had a meal together, same restaurant.' He smiled. 'We got teased by the waiter – he remembered us from Sunday night.'

'Aww, so sweet.' John laughed, and Mark joined in, looking so happy that Xan wanted to puke.

'So, I've asked her if we can meet up again this weekend, and I asked if she'd like to meet my friends.' He hesitated. 'Andy, would it be OK if I brought her to your place?'

Andy nodded. 'Yeah, we've got nothing

happening on Saturday and Helen will love it. Come round as early as you want, we won't do anything too formal.'

Mark breathed out, relieved, and looked round.

'Come on, guys, we've only got a couple of hours before Andy goes home. Bring me up to date with what you've been doing. I'm dying to get hold of a guitar again.'

Chapter 16

Mark had picked up on Xan's mood and chose to commute to the lakeside house from his mum's place, rather than stay over as he usually did. Xan had spent the night with Andy, crying his eyes out, unable to explain why the unconditional love that Andy and Helen gave him didn't quell the ache inside for someone who could be just his. It was the wolf thing; everything had been just fine until the wolf thing happened. Before the biting started, he'd been able to bitch with Andy about the weird amounts of privacy the Preston lads wanted. Now that Andy was a werewolf too, Xan felt horribly left out, and it didn't help that his early admiration for Mark's musical genius had turned into the worst case of infatuation he'd ever suffered from in his life.

He hadn't been left alone at all that week. Helen dropped by late on Wednesday night, ostensibly to borrow some videos, but really to check up on him. He'd been sitting alone, steadily drinking, and she'd led him to bed and got in with him, wrapping herself around him protectively. On Thursday night, Andy stayed after band practice, and on Friday night, again, Helen rang near midnight.

'Are you alone?' she asked.

'It's OK,' Xan said, calmer now. 'I don't need a pity fuck.'

Helen laughed, low and dirty. 'I do. Andy tired himself out with you last night, and I'm at the randy time of the month. He said he's going for a night hike with the Prestons; weird boys. Can I come round?'

'Sure,' Xan said, relieved but not admitting to it. 'I'd like that.'

She asked him, again, to move in with her and Andy, but it wouldn't have been right. They had a working relationship, the three of them, and while none of them doubted the love that they shared, the sex part of things was strictly paired off. Xan wasn't sure whose idea that had been originally, but suspected that it was Andy's, as he'd always been the most straitlaced of the three. If Xan moved into their home, things would change, and he might lose them both. That would kill him. Ah well, he thought, you take what you can get, and thankfully his relationship with the Ransomes wasn't his sole sexual outlet.

And then it was Saturday. Mark was playing it like he didn't have a fucking clue that Xan was in love with him, which was unbearably cruel. Hell, maybe he didn't, maybe he was that clueless? Xan had never told him, after all, not seriously. Every declaration of passion had been made in that sarcastic tone of voice that Xan couldn't help but use with Mark. Maybe Mark thought it was a running joke?

Xan arrived at the Ransomes' place early, and Helen went through her plans for a smooth introduction to Katie.

'Are you staying over?' she asked.

'I can't get through this thing sober,' Xan

replied. 'I'll go home if you want to drive me home?'

'You're staying here,' Helen said firmly. 'One of us could stay with you?'

Xan thought about it. The Ransomes had two guest rooms, one with a double bed, one with twins.

'I'm trying to be grown up. I'll share the twin room with John. OK?'

'Sure. I'll offer Katie the double bed, and Mark can take the sofa downstairs. It won't be the first time he's fallen asleep on it.'

Xan caressed Helen's face, appreciating her kindness. Mark and Katie would sleep together for the first time tonight, or not. Helen was working on the assumption that they wouldn't. He teased her. 'Or John and Mark can have the twin beds? I could bunk in with you and Andy, just for once. Like when we were all kids.'

'Before you seduced us, one after the other? Ah, Xan; no.'

'Meanie,' he said, sounding even more pathetic than he was aiming for, and shutting up.

He checked the clock. Still an hour to go until Mark and Katie arrived. He showered and put on a cologne that Mark had complimented him on once but not mentioned since. He wrapped a towel round himself and got to work on his hair and make-up. His hair was just too long to spike properly and he screamed in frustration; he couldn't get it right. Andy came in, looking ever so slightly annoyed.

'What now?' Andy asked.

Xan managed a moment of guilt; his scream had clearly interrupted something.

'I can't get my hair right,' he said, managing to sound appropriately subdued.

Andy rolled his eyes. 'Let me get dressed, I'll sort you out,' he said.

'Don't get dressed,' Xan said.

'Fuck you, Xan, if I don't get dressed we'll never get your hair sorted. Behave. You're acting like a child. This isn't about you, it's about Mark. Now, wash your hair while I get some jeans on.'

'Bossy git,' Xan whispered, but he washed the gunk out of his hair and combed it flat. He looked at his reflection, his naked face. His naked, ugly, unloveable face. Andy came in wielding a pair of scissors, a hairdryer and a make-up case.

'Shut your eyes,' he said.

'What are you going to do?'

'I'm going to make you irresistible to anyone who has the tiniest, slightest predilection for skinny blond men. If Mark doesn't gawp at you when he walks in tonight, it means that you should give up and behave. If he does gawp, I'm going to bloody well sabotage this Katie thing, OK?'

'You'd do that for me?' Xan asked.

'I'd die for you,' Andy said grimly. 'Don't ask me why, cos I don't have a fuckin' clue. Now, close your eyes.'

Xan kept his eyes closed, even when he felt Andy take his chin and lift his face up, and the spider tickle of the make-up.

'Done,' Andy said at last.

'Oh mama, you are gorgeous,' Xan told his reflection. His fine straight hair was roughly chopped into layers that drooped, but Andy had used just enough mousse to make it look naturally tousled. His grey-green eyes were flattered with a subtle green sheen on the eyelids – not full-blown eyeshadow, but a diluted colouring that drew attention to his eyes. The mascara was barely noticeable: subtle enough to be deniable, just enough to make a difference. The cold cream he'd felt at the start was depilatory; he'd not shaved for a couple of days, but his sparse stubble had gone, leaving his skin as smooth as a girl's. Andy had done an expert job with the eyeliner too, and the slightest hint of blusher emphasised his fine, high cheekbones.

'Jesus Christ, now I want to mess it all up,' Andy breathed. 'You just get dressed, they'll be here soon. Remember the deal, if he doesn't look twice at you, behave yourself.'

Even Xan saw the sense in that. He nodded.

Andy left, and Xan wriggled into his tightest jeans and a sleeveless red tee. He was admiring himself in the mirror when Helen came in and tied a red friendship bracelet around his left bicep, bestowing a delicate kiss to the bulge of his muscle. Xan felt a moment of displacement; this must be what a bride felt like, being prepared for the gaze of her beloved. Ah, but he wasn't a bride, he was just a pathetic overgrown kid making one last bid to catch the merest scrap of attention from the man he adored.

'I love you, Xan, but this is the last chance. If this doesn't work, you have to let him be,' Helen said.

'I know, and thank you for understanding,' he said. Her hair was down and she was dressed now, wearing a pretty, long-sleeved, full-length lilac dress with a high neckline. It was only when she stood in the light from the window that he realised that he could see straight through it to the lacy white underwear beneath. He grinned.

'Looking good, Hel.'

'Oh, I know.'

He made his way downstairs and took the seat opposite the living room door. John was already there, wearing khaki combat trousers and a dark green crew-neck jumper. Andy was setting the table, dressed very simply in blue jeans and a new white tee. There was a sense of nervousness and Helen put a CD on, leading to huge protests from all three men.

'Take That are banned in this house, you know that!' John yelled.

'Oh, but Mark Owen is so cute…' Helen said.

'Take. It. Off,' Andy croaked, holding his throat and writhing on the floor.

'Speaking of Marks,' Helen said, glancing out of the window, and everyone hurriedly composed themselves while Helen changed the CD to Fleetwood Mac's *Rumours.*

Mark didn't knock, he let himself in,

standing aside at the door to the living room to let Katie enter first. He glanced around the room, counting heads, his gaze settling with some puzzlement on Helen.

'She knows you can see though it, that's why she's wearing her best frillies,' Andy said, coming to Mark's rescue.

Xan managed to smile at Katie, who was looking at him in that half-confused way that celebrities quickly get used to.

'Do I know you?' she asked, politely. 'You seem familiar.'

Xan glanced at Mark and realised that his friend, the man he adored, was anxious. Xan suddenly understood: Mark had brought this woman to meet his friends and only now had he realised that he'd brought her to meet three attractive, charismatic men. He noticed that Xan looked wonderful, but interpreted it as rivalry, not seduction. Xan looked at Andy, and understood the warning look. They'd tried, and lost, and would bear it with grace.

Xan shrugged. 'My name's Xan Kendrick. I'm a musician, I get around. And you're a doctor – maybe you've treated someone who looks like me? Or maybe we've met in passing?'

Not a flicker of recognition now. Katie nodded.

'That'll be it.'

Xan had time to notice that she was wearing a designer sheath dress and matching shoes, but thankfully she wasn't carrying the matching handbag. The woman was a knockout: she had a fantastic body and carried herself very well. Mark was obviously a bloody fussy git, but when he'd finally made a move, he'd done spectacularly well.

Mark introduced John. 'My cousin, John Preston – we work together.' John bowed and kissed Katie's hand and looked at her flirtatiously. Katie blushed.

Mark was continuing with the introductions. 'My friends Helen and Andy Ransome. This is their home.'

Helen kissed Katie on the cheek. 'You're welcome to stay tonight. I've got a room ready for you, would you like to freshen up?'

Katie accepted, and was led upstairs by Helen. Mark glanced at Andy, questioning.

'We've got a room ready for her. You can share it or take the sofa, whatever,' Andy said, smiling. 'No pressure, mate.'

Mark understood. Helen would be tactfully making the situation clear to Katie too: the room was hers, and it was up to her whether or not she wanted company that night.

Katie came downstairs with Helen, all smiles, both of them making a real effort to be friendly.

Katie was nervous; she knew that she was missing something. Andy brought drinks for everyone, and said that dinner – a couple of pasta dishes and some salad – would be ready soon.

Mark took the seat next to Katie on the smaller of the two sofas, carrying a CD that he'd picked up from the huge rack in the corner of the room.

'This is our fourth album, our latest,' he said, handing it to her. She glanced at the cover, then around the room.

'I've heard of you,' she said at last. 'Mark, why didn't you tell me earlier?'

He shrugged. 'I wanted you to know me for myself, first. You're not a rock fan, so it wasn't really a conversation starter.'

'Are you in the band as well?' she asked Helen, who shook her head.

'The original plan was that I'd sing, Andy would play guitar, Xan would drum and we'd recruit a couple of guys for bass and rhythm guitar. Trouble was, we recruited Mark and John, so Andy moved to bass and I got cast out. I didn't mind, I was only playing along to please my boys anyway.' She leaned back into Andy's arms. 'I'm happy with things as they are, I enjoy my work.'

'What do you do?'

'I work at the interface between cell biology and biochemistry, on protein structures, interpreting the expression of genes. I love it.'

The conversation soon settled down. Helen was a skilled hostess, and carefully steered the lads away from the in-jokes that always threatened to take over any gathering where they were all present. Xan stayed quiet until he'd worked his way through an entire bottle of white wine, at which point he joined in, obviously subdued and contemplative. It was a long evening, and as it drew to a close, Katie relaxed against Mark, who awkwardly put his arm around her. He yawned, deliberately, and Helen exchanged an anxious look with Andy.

'It's never fair on the one sleeping on the sofa, is it? Come on, it's late, let's call it a night. Mark, you know where the spare bedding is. Katie, we don't set the burglar alarm, so if you want to get a drink or anything in the night, treat the kitchen as your own. Everyone else does. John, if you're going to snore, sleep in your car. Goodnight, everyone.' She took Andy's hand and hauled him to his feet. 'Xan, get yourself a pint of water to take to bed, eh?'

'Yes, Mum,' Xan whispered. He followed the others out of the room, casting a glance back to where Katie was lying against Mark, her eyes half closed.

He wanted to know, in a twisted, masochistic way, exactly what was going on down there. John was in the bathroom, brushing his teeth dutifully. Xan felt a moment of rage; there was no need for John to do that. He could Change twice and he'd be clean and perfect, gorgeous, smooth-skinned, and without those vile scars that proved that Xan was a complete failure. The door opened suddenly and John reached for the light switch, stopping when he saw Xan and the expression on his face.

'I'm sorry, mate,' he said, and Xan was angrier than ever, because John meant it. He pushed his way into the bathroom and stared at his face, rubbing violently at the make-up, using soap and water to take it all off, roughly towelling his face dry. He took a piss, and felt a childish urge to leave the toilet unflushed. Helen wouldn't like it, though, and he acted obediently, watching the water swirl away.

Katie was waiting outside with a pale pink towel and an overnight bag when he opened the door. She smiled at him, a little nervously.

'Oh, sorry, Alex, I wasn't sure if anyone was in there or not.'

'Xan,' he growled. 'Only my father calls me Alex.' And he stormed off to the spare room. John was pretending to be asleep.

Xan lay awake, waiting for the creak of the stairs that would signal either Mark coming upstairs or Katie going downstairs.

John whispered to him, 'Xan, go to sleep.'

'I can't,' Xan hissed. 'I'm miserable. I can't go to sleep when I'm miserable.'

'There's a notebook in my bag: write it down. I'm sure there's thousands of fifteen-year-olds out there who will identify with your pain and we might as well make some money out of it. Just do it quietly, will you?'

Xan was stunned by John's heartlessness, but couldn't stifle a giggle.

'You bastard. OK, I'll try to sleep.'

He dozed off eventually, but woke up again at three in the morning, wondering what had disturbed him. John was sat up, staring at him.

'Will you quit wailing?' he whispered.

'Nightmare, sorry,' Xan said, but the door had already opened.

John pulled the sheets over his head, giggling.

'We're in trouble now, you've woken Mum and Dad,' he said.

Helen sat on the edge of Xan's bed and whispered words he never thought he'd hear. He stood up and followed her towards the main bedroom.

Andy was sitting up, bleary-eyed.

'Xan, get in bed with us, special circumstances, eh? We didn't think you should be sleeping alone. Will you give up chasing Mark now?'

'Yes,' Xan said, getting into bed next to Andy and moving over so that he was between Andy and Helen. 'We've not all shared a bed since we were ten!'

'Just go to sleep,' Helen told him, turning away. He was asleep within seconds.

Chapter 17

He woke up when Helen got out of bed. She ignored his protests, making for the en-suite bathroom and closing the door behind her. Andy pulled him close and nibbled at his earlobe.

Xan laughed. 'What happened to the sanctity of the marriage bed?' he asked.

'We decided to give this a try, see how it goes. If you want to sleep with us, both of us, it's cool, but you gotta use condoms and give up fucking around. We need fidelity from you. And we don't stop the pairing-up thing, I don't want to lose my boyfriend completely in this threesome we've got going.'

'And I get to sleep with both of you together?' Xan asked.

'Sure.' Andy's breathing was faster. 'You were beautiful last night. Mark's a fool not to see it.'

'Katie's a bit of a babe actually,' Xan admitted. He pressed himself against Andy, squirming a little. Andy's teeth were against Xan's shoulder and he was moaning.

The bathroom door opened and they looked up at Helen. She put something on the bed and went back into the bathroom. Xan reached out.

'Durex, expired last month, but I'll risk it if you will? And spermicide cream, that'll do.' He peered at the tube. 'Expired last year? Are you two playing bareback these days? Hel never told me she was on the pill.'

'Babies,' Andy whispered. 'It's not

happening yet, but there's no reason why not.'

John was watchful at breakfast, aware of what had happened, asking each of the three in turn if they knew what they were doing. They told him that they did, and he relaxed. Mark and Katie were already up; they'd gone for a walk in the woods, evidently unaware of the events of the night before. When they returned, Mark made their excuses and they headed off back to Leeds. John left soon after, and by mid afternoon Xan was unsure enough of what was going on that he drove back to his own place to play some loud music.

The weeks rolled by, and eventually Mark moved into Katie's flat. Auntie Fran seemed upset until Mark told her that they'd already discussed marriage and were simply making sure it wouldn't be a mistake. Xan worked hard on overcoming his jealousy and being a good friend to Mark, but he couldn't like Katie, no matter how hard he tried. There was nothing specifically wrong with her, she just didn't gel with the gang. It would have been hard for anyone to, realistically, given how long they'd all been together. Mark seemed oblivious to the mild tension and just assumed that everyone would get along. The album took shape fast, with all four of the band members at peak creativity, and Xan's emotional roller coaster was producing lyrics that John's voice did full justice to.

Mark was careful to establish early on in his relationship that he wasn't going to be home every night. He needed to keep his freedom to run with John and Andy, and made it clear that it was entirely reasonable for him to spend the night at the Ransomes', or at Xan's, if they were working together. Katie was fine with the arrangement; she worked odd hours herself, and Mark's irregular hours made her feel less guilty. She was less understanding when they started talking about tour dates and tried to interfere with the arrangements. Mark talked about moving out and postponing the wedding, making it clear that this was non-negotiable, that band business had nothing to do with Katie and never would. Xan held his breath, waiting for the crack to become a split and the relationship to fall apart. It didn't. Katie saw sense, and the weekend before the tour kicked off, she and Mark threw a housewarming party.

Andy had agreed to drive, and knocked on the door to pick up Xan. He could see Helen, who was already in the car, looking anxious, and glancing at the two men. Xan picked up his keys and looked at Andy.

'What's wrong, babe?' he asked.

'Tonight. It's not our kind of party, OK? Can you be discreet about the three of us?'

Xan blinked, understanding immediately. This party was a celebration of Mark and Katie's relationship, it would be an ordeal that he needed help to get through, and Andy and Helen wanted to disown him? He couldn't see how anything could be worse.

'Discreet? You mean turn up as Mr and Mrs Ransome plus Billy No Mates? Fuck you.' He shut the door in Andy's face, and watched as his oldest friend walked away. Helen met him halfway up the path, protesting, and Andy turned away.

The doorbell rang again, insistently, but there was no response. Helen decided to use her key. She found him on the bed, staring at the ceiling.

'I bet he phrased it badly?' she said tentatively. 'We want you to come, but for Mark's sake, we don't want to upset Katie. She doesn't understand what we have.'

'We have nothing,' Xan spat.

'Brat.' Helen sat on the edge of the bed. The silence grew.

'This isn't working, is it?' Xan said eventually.

'No.' Helen didn't spare him. 'No, it's not. I'm glad we tried, but it's not working. I was happy with it, until I caught on to how Andy feels.'

Xan pulled her closer. 'He's jealous. I can't believe it. After all these years, he's jealous of us. Why not before, when we were couples? He was never jealous then, was he?'

'He's got worse as he's got older. Most men do.' Helen kissed Xan's forehead. 'Maybe as long as we were just coupling up, he could pretend that although he was fucking both of us, me and thee were just getting together to play Scrabble? He can't hide from the truth when we're all in the same bed. He actually asked me who I preferred, last night. He's not asked that since we were fifteen.'

Xan realised that he was crying. 'Will he make you choose?' he asked.

'Nobody is going to get dumped. Not me,

not you, not him.' Helen stroked his face. 'I won't give you up, ever. We have to find a way to get back to where we were.'

Xan wiped his eyes. 'I was getting fed up of monogamy anyway, or digamy, or whatever it is. I've been faithful to you two for ages now, it was driving me mad.' He kissed her, hungry for comfort. 'I'm not coming to the party. I'll bet that Katie's matched the girl / boy numbers exactly, and I don't want to be forced into entertaining some middle-aged chiropodist.'

'Please, Xan, go with Andy. Make things up with him. I hate it when the two of you quarrel. I'll stay here. How does that sound?' Helen smiled carefully, but Xan knew when her heart was breaking and he held her tightly, wishing he could have been the man she deserved.

A deeper voice spoke. Andy stood in the doorway, leaning on the frame.

'It sounds like a good idea to me.' He was biting his lip. 'Helen's right, nobody's going to get dumped, 'specially as I've got a strong suspicion that it'll be the big bad jealous guy who goes, if anyone does. I'm sorry, both of you, I just can't handle this any more. I can't take the three-in-a-bed deal. I thought I could cope, but I can't. I'm mad at Helen when she touches Xan, and Xan when he touches Helen. It's not like that for you guys, you enjoy watching me with the other one, you love it when we're all together. I'm just too possessive.'

Xan stood up, bending to kiss Helen again, just to make the point that he could and he would.

'I'll wash my face and fix my hair. Come on, Ransome, we've got a party to liven up.'

He went into the bathroom and Andy looked at Helen.

'I'll sleep alone tonight. I'll drop him off here. You'll be alone too much anyway when we tour.'

Helen nodded. 'Look after him at the party.'

Andy smiled sadly and left, waiting downstairs for Xan.

Chapter 18

Tour time. The band believed in touring hard, and would rather play a medium-sized venue three times than a soulless arena once. Xan locked up his house, asked Helen to check on it now and again and hit the road. Japan first, then a couple of weeks in the US and Canada, doing the college towns, then a fortnight in Rio, where Helen joined them. Rio was mostly R&R, but the two gigs they did play were sell-outs. The album hit the charts in the top five and crept up slowly. By the time they got back to Europe it was number one, and had been for three weeks. The first single had crawled into the top five. The second went top three in the first week. The Ransomed Hearts knew that they had a following wind, and Andy was worn out, playing and partying at night, and negotiating hard with suppliers and venues during the day.

'More merch. Different sized T-shirts, badges, sweatbands, baseball caps, mugs!' he demanded, seeing kids and grandparents in the queue before the doors opened. He suggested a merch catalogue to be given out as people left the venue, as not everyone had the time or energy to wrestle through a scrum to the T-shirt concession. Money poured in, the tour made a profit, their label was ecstatic and sales went through the roof. Xan registered that they were top of the shit heap again. They got to the UK in October, adding more dates. Xan begged for a rest and was excused all promo duties. He slept all day, and came out at night to bang his drums and be seen at the parties. The third single went straight to number one. Andy didn't forget their friends, organising a mailshot to all the people who'd been on the fan club mailing list back in the eighties, when they first got started. They'd finish the tour in mid-December and give Mark back to Katie for Christmas, but first they'd play a thank-you gig for their first fans, in Manchester.

It was deliberately informal: Helen, who never forgot a face, walked down the specially invited queue outside the venue, handing out tickets. She watched the crowd afterwards, and only eight of them sold their tickets on immediately. Mark sent his guitar tech out to ask how much the tickets had gone for.

'Two hundred and fifty,' the woman reported back, amazed.

The last gig was almost all acoustic, to suit the room; a singalong, a celebration of all the time the band and these loyal fans had been together. They signed everything and anything afterwards.

'Where's Katie?' Xan asked, eventually, when the crowd was dying down.

'She's got a black-tie dinner to go to, wanted me to go with her.' Mark shook his head. 'I told her I'd be home for a few months now, plenty of time for me to get into the surgeon's husband routine.'

Xan smiled, everything forgiven now. The tour was over and he could spend a few weeks rediscovering the pleasures of home. He and Andy had been discreet, on the tour, but they'd found time for each other, and Helen had spent as much time in Rio with Xan as she had with Andy. Andy was clear that out of sight was out of mind for him, and the three of them seemed to be happy now. Xan's heart still ached for Mark, and he knew of no way to get over him, but his love outweighed his desire and he hid his feelings. The thought of Mark Preston at a black-tie dinner, making small talk with consultants and politicians, was delightfully amusing, but he knew that Mark could deal with it, and would. Mark's mother had brought him up well, and he'd spent enough time in the music business to be able to deal with all kinds of people.

The five of them spent the night in John's Manchester flat, Mark bunking in with his cousin, Andy taking the sofa, and Helen and Xan squashed into the queen-sized guest bed. John could afford a bigger flat, but hated the thought of moving.

The next morning Xan and Helen headed back to Xan's place. Xan understood that it was time for wolf business, and he distracted Helen with pretty promises, leaving Andy with the Prestons. Something had happened on that tour: he'd become sated with the adulation of the crowds, and it was finally enough. He'd relaxed enough to drop the sarcastic tone he usually used with Mark and John, and was surprised to find that they instantly responded to his changed attitude, spending more time with him. How much had he pissed them off over the years? How much must they love him to have tolerated the crap he put them through? Taking Helen out of the picture for the night was the least he could do for them. He smiled. Taking

Helen out of the picture for the night would be a pleasure.

She'd made sure that his home was ready for his return: the gardens were neat and tidy, the fridges and freezer were stocked and everything was clean. His bedroom was aired, the bed made. They had done it together, smoothing the sheets, putting the pillowcases on, watching every move the other made. When their bed was ready, he undressed slowly, for her pleasure, making sure that when his kecks came off, he had an erection that complimented her thoroughly. She undressed slowly, teasing him, and when she was down to bra and knickers he pulled her on to the bed and caressed her. They made love with long familiarity, and afterwards they talked about success and love and how wonderful it was to still be together.

'If I'd married you, Andy would have left us,' Helen said, out of nowhere.

Xan considered it, and reluctantly agreed. He pinched Helen's nipple, not entirely gently.

'But you married *him,* and we're all still together,' he pointed out.

She retaliated in kind, and he grunted and tried to roll her on to her back, but she laughed and fought back. A body toned by tennis and swimming fought against one habituated to parties, fucking and playing the drums for hours every day. Xan won, and pinned her against the bed, looking into her blue eyes – the same blue as Andy's. He felt her long legs wrap around him, and surrendered in victory.

Chapter 19

Diana laughed, eyes shut tight, as a swirl of wind-driven sleet hit the scarf that she'd wrapped round her
face. She'd soon be home. Warm yellow light spilled through the transom window above her front door and she felt a shiver of anticipation at the thought of the night to come. These were the best nights: cold, wet and windy, when anyone with any sense stayed home. Diana had other plans, but they were for later.

The house was warm, bright and empty. She left her wet coat and boots in the hallway, prepared a meal, and settled down at the kitchen table with the radio on. Someone was reviewing demo tapes from new bands, and after she'd finished eating and clearing up she turned the volume down and let the sound of music and conversation wash over her as she worked on some stats for her research. At 11 pm she switched the house lights off and used a lamp to illuminate her work. She felt no need for sleep, but the urge to Change had been growing strong for days now. It was time. Outside, a waxing moon illuminated a pavement alive with bouncing rain and Diana found herself distracted by thoughts of prowling the back alleys of north Manchester; of tearing the bitter, sinewy throat out of the biggest rat she could find.

She Changed in the back garden, in a sheltered corner she knew wasn't overlooked, and took a running leap over the high wall and into the back street. She prowled for half a mile before she found an unwary rat and killed it with one swift shake. It was gone in two bites, and she moved north, heading towards the suburbs and the moors beyond. Among the fields she ran, stretching her legs in joy at the glorious freedom that she so loved. Soon, she was in the hills, clambering among the rocks, hungry for something new. A scattered flock of sheep was of no interest to her, and she cautiously retreated from an underground den when she realised it was filled with sleepy badgers. A young fox had run from her at first, and then cautiously watched her from afar until she gave the universal canine signal for play, bowing swiftly to it. They enjoyed a wild game of chase until the fox grew tired. She sat and turned her back, letting it wander away to hunt and rest. She found an injured rabbit trying desperately to hide, and quickly killed and ate it, carefully leaving the badly damaged leg to one side because it smelled bad. She was stalking a weasel for the sheer fun of it when twin howls split the night and she froze. These voices were unknown. She was downwind of them, and estimated they were between five and ten miles away.

She hesitated. She certainly wasn't looking for company, but she did want to know more about these strangers. She circled around, running fast and low, staying downwind as much as she could. She saw a parked vehicle on a farm track and crept closer to investigate. She picked up the scent of wolves and humans, and established that a group of three men had left the vehicle; two had Changed and one had walked away. The vehicle was locked, but she sniffed the key out, tucked out of sight on the windscreen, held in place by one of the wipers. She retreated and waited.

When two black wolves appeared over the ridge she found herself holding her breath. They trotted back to the vehicle and Changed, both of them stretching and yawning as they found their human shapes. The slimmer guy opened the boot and handed a bundle of clothes to his companion, and took out another pile for himself. Diana crept closer, confident that they couldn't smell or hear her in their human form. There was something very familiar about the two men and she wanted to get closer, to hear what they were saying. The wind had been her friend so far, but now it was making it impossible to hear anything. A sudden gust brought a new scent, one that she instinctively found terrifying. Big cat. She turned and saw a leopard crouching above her, about to spring. She yelped in fright and leaped to her feet, running fast towards her own kind, and she hoped towards safety. The two werewolves by the car stepped back in surprise when they saw her. She jumped up on to the vehicle and growled, low and vicious, as the leopard approached. Its skin rippled and it Changed, leaving a tall, blond man gazing up at her. He spoke.

'Well, who the hell are you?'

The skinny guy threw a third bundle of clothes at the naked blond. 'Ransome: whoever it is you've obviously freaked them out.'

Diana blinked. Ransome? Ah, now she knew. She Changed and jumped down from the roof of the vehicle, almost losing her balance. Mark Preston moved forwards to steady her, then stepped back, unsure. She grinned.

'Hey lads, where's your drummer?'

Ten minutes later she was sat in the back seat of the car, wearing Andy Ransome's long T-shirt and John Preston's denim jacket, listening to Mark Preston's somewhat rambling account of how he and John were cousins and had been werewolves since they were boys, and how Xan had eventually discovered their secret. How Mark and John had decided to see if the old legends were true by biting Xan and Andy to try to infect them. How it had worked for Andy, but not Xan. Diana decided that Mark was sharing information far too fast, and decided not to disclose her own history in too much detail. She was, she said, the only child of two teachers, brought up in the North East and now a senior research assistant in genetics at the University of Manchester. Andy commented that his wife was working in a similar field, under her maiden name, and Diana confirmed that she'd heard of Dr Helen Townsend and was impressed by her work. A few more questions revealed that Helen was unaware of the 'werewolf thing' and that the men were committed to keeping her firmly in the dark. Diana found that interesting, and a relief.

'So, is there a Mr Diana?' Mark asked. Diana turned her attention to him. Five six, maybe five seven, wiry, with seriously gorgeous long black hair, intense dark eyes and slender features dominated by a long, thin nose. She shrugged.

'No, there never really seemed to be any point, I don't need that complication.'

'I get it.' Mark nodded. 'I've been waiting for you all my life. I mean, someone like you, someone like us.'

In the front of the car, John and Andy exchanged a look; they seemed to be simultaneously amused and exasperated. Andy spoke up.

'It's getting light, I don't know what arrangements you have to get home…?'

Diana shrugged. 'I'm usually home well before dawn, I jump the wall and the back door isn't locked. I'm not sure if I can get over the wall in this particular body though – I'm a bit short…'

'You're just fine.' Mark smiled.

Andy coughed. 'Look, tell us where you live, and we'll drop you off, help you over the wall. And we'll keep in touch, what do you think?'

'Sounds good.' Diana nodded. She was distracted; Mark's eyes were fascinating, deep brown pools that drew her in and captivated her. She was half amused by her own reaction; this physical attraction was something new to her, and she wasn't sure how to deal with it. Really, she thought, she should have got all this stuff out of her system when she was a teenager. 'Oh, yes … my address.'

John knew the area, and navigated while Andy drove. Mark was quiet, looking out of the window, then at Diana, then out of the window again.

'You clearly know who we are...' he said eventually.

'Yeah, got all your albums. Just vinyl, I've not got round to replacing them with CDs yet. I like rock music, you know? I recognised you from the album art. I'm afraid I've never been to a gig, and I don't really follow the music press. I mean, I read *Sounds* when I was a teenager, now and again, but I'm not really musical myself.' She smiled. 'You have great hair.'

Mark smiled. 'Thank you.'

'Oh, all of you have. Is it a Shifter thing?'

'Shifter?'

'Shapeshifter, Shifter. It's how I think of myself. And now I've seen what Ransome can do, it's kind of obvious that "werewolf" doesn't work.'

Mark shrugged. 'Andy had great hair before we infected him, so no, I don't think so. I kinda like your hair too.'

Diana took a breath. How old was she? This conversation should have happened when she was fifteen years younger.

'Thank you,' she managed.

Chapter 20

Diana had to admit that the guys had good instincts. They drove the car slowly down the back street behind her house, and she easily got over the wall by standing on the top of the car. She heard the car move away and bit her lip, wondering what came next. Should she contact them or wait for them to get in touch? She let herself into the house and locked the back door, leaning against it with her eyes closed. She smiled and walked through the house. She needed a shower; her feet were filthy and she had bits of heather in her hair and splashes of peaty mud on her arms and legs. That leap from the top of the car had been more ungainly than she'd have liked. Not a good way to make a first impression.

She was halfway up the stairs when she heard a quiet knock at the front door. She swallowed. Nobody visited her, ever, and it was too early for the post. She skipped down the steps and opened the door a crack.

'Yeah?' she said to Mark.

'Um, yeah, the guys say to keep the clothes, as long as you need them.' Mark shrugged.

'I do have clothes.' Diana smiled. 'But that's nice of them.'

'Look, can we talk? I mean, it's OK if you just want to give us your phone number or…'

Diana opened the door and waved Mark through.

'Put the kettle on. I was just about to have a

shower. Where are the others?'

'They went back to John's flat, it's in the city centre. They'll pick me up later.' He smiled. 'Do you know that you've got heather in your hair?'

'Maybe it'll bring me luck.' Diana grinned, then blushed. 'I didn't mean…'

'Oh, hell no. I didn't think…' Mark laughed. 'I've thought so much about what would happen if I ever met a woman like me, like us, and here you are…'

Diana stared at him. They were close together in the narrow hallway and Mark was showing no signs of heading to the kitchen. She swallowed.

'Here I am. Um, about that cuppa?' She waited for him to move, but he was staring at her. It was unnerving, those eyes of his had her trapped.

'Are they real? Your eyes?' Mark asked her.

'What?'

'I mean, they're so green, I've never seen eyes like that before. Are they contacts or something?'

'When have I had time to put contacts in? I've still got twigs in my hair!'

'Um, yeah.' He reached out to pluck a particularly large sprig of heather from the top of her head, and she raised her hand to stop him.

'Don't, I'll do it.' Diana said quietly. Their hands were touching, and she took his hand in hers and moved it away from her hair. 'It's pretty much stuck, don't pull…'

Mark bit his lip. 'Well, I just thought we

could talk, maybe? But this is awkward. I mean, we're strangers and… I'll ring John's flat, ask him to come back for me. Can I wait in the kitchen?'

'Sure.' Diana led him into the kitchen, it was freezing cold and she turned the electric heater on before switching on the kettle and getting teabags from the cupboard. 'Milk? Sugar? And you'll be hungry, I've got bacon and eggs in the fridge.'

'May I?' Mark moved to the fridge. 'Cooking is the least I can do after we messed up your run.'

'Well, I don't meet Shifters every day, do I?'

'You've met others?'

There was a pause. Diana smiled. 'Nope, but I guessed I couldn't be the only one. How did you guys meet?'

She listened as they prepared food and drink, nodding sagely when he told her again that Mark and John were cousins, and making mental notes when he told her about infecting Andy, and about trying and failing to infect Xan. They demolished bacon, eggs, toast, cereal and a pint of tea each while talking. Then Diana shook her head.

'Look, I'm still muddy and full of twigs – give me a minute or two to tidy up?' She stood up, and bent to kiss him on the forehead. 'You're very sweet, thank you for cooking breakfast.' He raised his face and the kiss landed awkwardly on his nose. 'Whoops!' Diana laughed, and was still laughing when Mark drew her face down to his and kissed her gently on the lips. She drew away and stared at him, licking her lips. 'That tingles. Does it always tingle?' She didn't wait for an answer, bending down to kiss him again. This time it was a deep kiss, and she moaned as he stood up and embraced her.

'Is this OK?' Mark muttered.

'Yes,' Diana whispered. 'Don't stop.'

At some point they moved upstairs, to the bedroom at the back of the house where Diana kept her clothes and where she sometimes slept. At some point she'd lost the T-shirt and jacket, and Mark was kicking his jeans off and hurriedly peeling his socks away. As she drew him to her, he closed his eyes.

'I have a girlfriend,' he muttered. 'I shouldn't…'

'Do you want to?' Diana asked. She rolled away from him and waited.

'Yes.'

'Well, so do I. It doesn't mean forever, does it?' She smiled as he groaned and pulled her towards him again.

Mark broke away. 'Have you drugged me?'

'What are you talking about?'

'This, it's overwhelming, it's crazy, I can't think, it's never been like this before. You're on fire…' he sighed. They fell together into a blaze of heat and light, their bodies tangled, intertwined, one.

He was weeping. 'You are mine, aren't you? You'll always be mine…' he whispered.

'Always,' Diana promised.

They slept for a while and woke hungry for each other. They stayed together all day, and all the next night, barely registering hunger or thirst, fitfully sleeping for minutes before waking up to a desperate, mutual need. When they were too exhausted to fuck, they exchanged life stories, although Diana remained circumspect about her own family. He talked about his mother, his lost father, his cousin and his friends. Eventually, realising how much time had passed, he haltingly brought up Katie. He recognised that this was not something that Diana wanted to hear, but she deserved to hear the truth. And the truth was that he was not free to love Diana as he wanted to. Diana understood what he was capable of giving her, and what he was willing to give her, but the gap between the two was destroying her even as he held her so close that she felt his heart beating against her chest. Could she accept this? Was it all she deserved?

He stood at the window and watched the sun rise. 'Another day. I have to go. Katie will be worried. This isn't like me. I don't do this sort of thing.'

He looked down at himself and saw that his body was scratched and scarred, but knew it would heal fast. He was exhausted, but all he wanted was Diana. He tore himself away and rang John. When he left, Diana stared at the ceiling. She knew that he would be back. She knew that they weren't finished.

The pain kicked in about half an hour after he left. It started as a mild headache, combined with a hungry ache that wasn't assuaged by food or water. It built up slowly, and it took her a couple of hours to realise what was happening. As her guts clenched and rejected food, her brain refused to be distracted by TV or computer games or books. Every part of her body was telling her that it hurt to be away from Mark, demanding his return. The only comfort was to lie in bed, curling up in the space he'd occupied for so long, trying to remember every detail of their hours together, crying his name and wondering where he was, what hold the outside world could exert to take him away from her.

By evening, exhausted and furious, she decided to try to eat. She dragged herself out of bed and staggered downstairs. In the mirror on the landing her bone-white face stared out from a frame of lank red hair. Her eyes were slits, lost in a pool of shadows. As she got to the bottom of the stairs, she saw a dark shape outlined against the glass of the front door. A figure, sitting slumped on the step. She tapped on the glass and he jumped up. It was John. Diana opened the door, and John smiled cautiously, offering her a bedraggled bunch of red roses and a large brown carrier bag.

'Your bell doesn't work. And I think you've gone deaf, because I've been knocking for half an hour. Can I come in?'

He marched past her and opened the bag. 'Chinese food. Is that OK? It's still warm.' Diana stared as he rooted through the cupboards, found two plates and dished out piles of food. He let her sit down and followed suit. She pushed the food away and waited for him to say something.

He took a deep breath. 'Mark's in a bad

state. Worse than you are. Katie's having a fit, she doesn't know what's wrong with him. He was screaming your name when I went round. Fortunately she didn't hear that. He's at my flat now. What the hell happened? It's like he's going cold turkey. Andy's looking after him. I was trying to help, and I thought that you might be in trouble too.'

He noticed that she looked nauseous and took her plate away.

'Look, there's something very wrong with both of you. Is there anything I can do to help?' He saw that she was sweating and pale, and as she fell forwards he moved fast and caught her. She twisted in his arms and threw herself to the floor, looking up at him with utter disgust.

'What the fuck was that?' she groaned. He was genuinely upset, and came closer. She flinched. Whatever had been started between Mark and Diana was vehemently rejecting John's presence.

'Don't you want me around? Mark told me you'd agreed to join us.' He kneeled on the floor next to her. He sounded truly distressed.

'I don't know what's happening to me. I just know that it's almost too powerful for me right now. I'm terrified. Please, I need Mark, I can't eat or drink or sleep without him. Can you take me to him?'

He reached out again, pure sympathy in his eyes, then drew back in frustration.

'Damn, I want to hold you. I couldn't stay away from you,' he said. 'I've wanted to be near you since I first saw you.'

'Are you flirting?' Diana asked, incredulous. She looked at the roses lying next to the sink, visibly wilting now.

He blinked, confused. 'I don't know. I want to help you, but I need to be close to you. It's not sex. I just want to be with you, look after you.' Their eyes met and Diana relaxed. She understood.

They moved to the living room, sitting on the big sofa and facing each other, their feet almost touching, keeping that careful balance between the need to be together and the pain that Diana knew would hit her if they touched.

'If you won't take me to Mark, talk to me about him,' she whispered.

John frowned, then his face cleared. Diana could see him arranging the story in his mind, step by step, as he must have rehearsed it many times. He glanced at her to make sure he had her attention and started to tell his story.

They'd been fourteen, adolescent and full of dreams. They were friend, cousins, as close as brothers, and they were determined to be musicians. They would jam together several times a week, getting progressively stricter and more disciplined. For at least nine months, John had noticed a fierce anger in Mark, hidden behind his neat, well-behaved exterior, an urge to strike out against the world, a loneliness that he could not reach. It came out in the music, and John knew they had something real. They were looking for a drummer, a lyricist, another guitarist, but were waiting for the right people to appear. It had never occurred to them that sometimes the right people don't appear.

A day had come when John had lost patience with Mark's moodiness. He'd felt unsettled himself, and had little time for his cousin's refusal to open up. After asking him, yet again, what was wrong, he'd walked out. It only took a minute or two for him to run home, and he banged the back door behind him as he stormed into the house. His mother had been in the kitchen and had called to him as he'd run up the stairs to his small bedroom. He closed the door, more gently. The room was too small. In truth, the town was too small for him, and he threw himself to the bed, struggling to make sense of the burning fury that was growing inside him. He'd remembered agonising pain, an angry confusion, and nothing more until he was lying weeping in Mark's arms.

Mark had told him about his own first Changes, about the loneliness of suddenly realising that he was the only one it happened to, and how he'd forced away despair by treating his difference as a challenge, an experiment. Within weeks, Mark could change from human to wolf and back at will. Even if John hadn't been true kin to him, and another Shapeshifter, Mark would have survived. He had steel in his soul.

Mark had recognised the growing fury in John over the last few months and had watched him, hoping that it wasn't merely teenage angst. John hadn't realised that he was actually growling as he walked out on Mark that night, but Mark had blinked once in recognition then followed his cousin home, keeping to the shadows. He'd followed John into the house, seeing the first stages of the Change begin even as John ran upstairs. Miriam, John's mother, had been following John, but Mark got between her and the stairs.

'We had a row, I'll sort him out,' he explained, pushing past her, opening the bedroom door and locking it behind him. His aunt banged on the door furiously, panicked by the eerie howls and crashing noises, then gave up. She shook her head, trying to remember a similar outburst of fury from her own teenage years, and failing. Inside the room, Mark was hugging a powerful black wolf, trying to force it to the floor. He didn't want to Change, not in a locked room with his unpredictable cousin. He was surprised to find that he felt no fear, just an overwhelming ache of mixed joy and sorrow for John and himself. At last, he felt John's muscles writhe beneath him, fur disappear, claws retract, and he was lying on the floor, his naked cousin in his arms. John was shaking and crying.

John finished the story. 'You see, if Mark hadn't been looking out for me, my mother would have found me like that … who knows what would have happened? I owe him a lot. He taught me everything he knew, everything he'd learned since his first Change. That's when he realised that if there were two of us, there must be more, and we've been searching ever since. Being in the band helps, we get around the country. We run whenever we get chance, but this is the first time we've ever found anyone.'

Diana considered his story, glad of the distraction. 'So your fathers are brothers? Do you think they were Shifters?'

John looked away. It wasn't something he was comfortable about discussing.

'Perhaps. We were very young when they went away and we've not heard anything from them since. Our mothers definitely aren't, we'd know.'

She could reassure him on that point. 'Well, the trait is recessive, I know that much. Your mothers must be carriers. Your fathers could be carriers, or full-blooded Shapeshifters like us. Perhaps one of each?

John shook his head. 'I don't know. Mum's dead now, but she didn't talk about my dad, and my aunt refuses to talk about Mark's dad.'

'Andy?' she asked, dropping the subject of the cousins' ancestry.

'No, we definitely made him, like we told you. You've heard all those stories about lycanthropy being transmitted by bites? We decided to see if it was true. It worked with Andy, eventually. We've known him and Xan since we all met at sixth form. Mark insisted on giving both of them the chance to be wolf as well as in the band; the two things are entwined in his mind. He's amazing, everyone thinks he's the quiet muso, but without him we wouldn't exist as a band, and I doubt I'd even be alive.'

He paused and looked at Diana, 'I get all the attention these days … lead-singer syndrome I suppose … and I suppose I half expected you to be interested in me, the other morning, not Mark. But I've thought about it, and I think you're right.'

Diana shrugged, not understanding. The pain returned, worse than ever, and John understood why she flinched. He held out his hand to her, but she shook her head. She desperately needed comfort, but the sickness wouldn't allow her to touch or be touched by John. 'He'll come as soon as he can, you know,' John told her. He looked into her eyes and saw the despair.

'Tell me about his girlfriend. Tell me about Katie.' Diana's voice was controlled and low. John looked at the table for a while before starting to speak.

'Well, you have to understand, Mark isn't like me. I've always been a bit of a lad. Ever since I realised what I was, I couldn't take any relationship seriously. It fits in with the rock-star image. I've lost count of the number of women I've slept with, but I've probably only had one or two girlfriends, and even with them, I wouldn't commit. Don't get me wrong, I like women, I just find it hard to find someone who understands me. I don't think I could ever be happy with just one woman for the rest of my life. Mark is different. Even when we were teenagers, he seemed to be keeping himself for someone. I laughed at him, but, well, he's pretty stubborn.'

'Go on,' Diana said.

'Can you believe he was still a virgin when he met Katie? It wasn't for lack of attention either, the girls were all over the four of us. Then one day earlier this year, he brought her to Andy and Helen's place to meet us. He'd met her in the bloody park, of all places, where she was reading a book about fractal art, which he's interested in, and they got talking. They didn't sleep together for weeks, he kept telling me that. I think he wanted points for good behaviour. Then one night he came round to mine, got drunk and asked me if I seriously thought there were any other werewolves around. I had to say I didn't. We'd been touring for years already, running as wolves in dozens of towns and cities, different countries, and never found anyone. He had a few more drinks then went to Katie's. I think he started the relationship in desperation, but he genuinely loves her now.'

John hesitated before he hit her with it. 'No one else knows but Andy, Xan and me … he proposed to her and they're getting married in September.'

Diana stood, walked to a cupboard and took out a bottle of whisky and a glass. John watched her down the first two glasses, and then gently took the bottle away.

'That won't help,' he told her.

'Tell me the rest,' she demanded.

He brushed his curls away from his face.

'When we left here yesterday, we went back to my flat first. He told me that he's angry with himself for making a commitment to Katie, but says it's too late, he loves her too much now. I asked him if he could give you up, but he said it was impossible, that you were in his blood. Look, you need to know. If Mark says something, he sticks by it. You can't have him to yourself. But I don't think he can stay away from you either.'

Diana nodded. 'I'm going back to bed.'

He followed her upstairs. 'I'll sit up with you, you're not fit to be alone.'

He was as good as his word, and while she got a few hours of fitful sleep, he brought a chair into the bedroom and sat up, watching her, whispering soothing words when she called out Mark's name in her delirium.

At eight the next morning, he gently woke her up, his long hair brushing her face.

'Sweetheart, there's someone here.' Diana opened her eyes. Andy was standing in the doorway, supporting Mark, who looked dreadful.

Andy glared at John. 'Well, she looks better than he does,' he said accusingly. 'I had to bring him, he's not eaten anything and all he does is cry out for her.'

Mark opened his eyes and staggered forwards, Diana leaped out of bed in a second and caught him in her arms. He reached out and blindly held her. John and Andy exchanged a long look and left the room. Diana couldn't support Mark's weight, and lowered him to the floor. He reached up and kissed her hungrily, and once again the wild took them. He held her tightly, whispering her name.

'I can't stay away from you. This can't be right, how are we supposed to live like this?'

'Could you touch Katie? Could you hold her?' Diana drew away from another deep kiss to ask him.

'Yes,' he whispered. 'But I didn't want to, I want you.'

Half an hour of kisses refreshed the couple to the point that they started to feel hungry, so they made their way downstairs to forage for food.

Andy and John hadn't left, and stopped talking when the lovers walked into the kitchen. John cooked breakfast, throwing stuff on to plates and putting it in front of them. They didn't break their grip on each other's hands, eating one-handed. John sat opposite them, watching, openly relieved. Andy glared at Mark and Diana. He looked like he wanted to make a speech. Diana looked expectantly at him until he started.

'I didn't want to be part of this. I'm married. I don't need another woman. And the wolf business is hard enough on Xan without someone else joining us, someone else who is something he can never be. But … I can feel what's going on here, and I can't stay away from it. I want to be near her–' he refused to look at Diana – 'just as much as you two do. But I need to know what we're letting ourselves in for. I need to know something about who you are.'

He finally looked at Diana directly. She shrugged, told him about her parents, about finding out what she was, about getting support from them – John and Mark looked shocked at that point. She told them about being lucky enough with inheritances from sickly relatives to be able to buy the house she lived in. She didn't tell them about the other women; she certainly didn't tell them about her sister. Something, some protective instinct, warned her not to. Finally, she told them about her job, her research.

Andy interrupted. 'I need to know what you want from us.'

Diana shrugged. 'I want Mark. I want to spend the rest of my life with the three of you. I want a family, with kids who will grow up to be like us. It's the only thing that makes any sense to me right now.'

He nodded. 'That's what I can't deal with. I'm married. I can't be part of that.'

Mark looked at Diana. 'You're right, that's what I need more than anything. I need all of you, you're all part of me now. But I won't leave Katie. I've made promises to her, and I won't break them.'

Diana turned to John.

'I'm happy with whatever makes you happy,' he assured her. He reached out and touched her face. Somehow, with Mark there, it was OK.

Chapter 21

Andy kept out of Xan's way for the next few days. He had seemed anxious, and disappeared without warning, saying only that he was going to see Mark. John wasn't returning any phone calls, and Mark was completely off the map.

Eventually he got through to Katie, who was clearly terrified. Mark hadn't come home as expected; he'd been out of touch for several days, and when he had returned he'd acted very strangely, become delirious and seemed to be in pain. She'd been about to call for an ambulance when Andy had arrived, clearly summoned by Mark, and bundled the guitarist into his car and driven him away. She'd not seen or heard from anyone since, and was panicked and furious.

'If he's with Andy, he's safe,' Xan said, amazed at how firm his voice was. 'And I can't contact John either, so whatever's going on, he's involved too. Neither of them will let any harm come to Mark, I promise you that. Don't you understand by now? We're solid.'

'So why don't you know what's going on?' Katie snapped, slamming the phone down.

Xan paled, then flushed. He knew what was going on: it was wolf business. Nobody knew what price the Shifting powers would exact, nobody had ever even wondered about it, but perhaps this was some illness that John and Andy understood. They were clearly keeping Mark out of the reach of the medical profession, and must have had a very good reason if they were willing to piss Katie off.

Andy came home early in the morning and apologised to Helen, but gave no explanations. Helen had given him a wise look and decided not to push it; the comedown from a tour could be heavy, and she'd lived through some wild times. The Ransomes went to Xan's for lunch, and while they were there, Katie rang Helen, threatening to set the law on Andy. Katie's suspicions were that Andy and John had lured her trusting, innocent fiancé into a drug-fuelled orgy. Not only that, but he'd disappeared again, and she wanted to know where to.

Xan managed a smile, but caught Andy's eye while Helen progressively lost her temper with Katie.

'Look, the five of us have been friends since we were teenagers. None of us would hurt Mark. If they took him away, it was for his protection. If he doesn't trust you, yelling about it won't help, will it? You've got to get used to the fact that he's not just yours. If you can't deal with that, cancel the fucking wedding.' She slammed the phone down and turned to Xan, furious.

'I wanted him to find someone, but did it have to be her?'

Xan, for once, played peacemaker. 'Come on, Hel, anyone would be worried about what happened. I'm worried myself, but at least we know that we can trust Andy and John. Let it be, it's over.'

Helen glanced at Andy, anxious now she knew that Mark had been ill. Andy shrugged.

'We went on a bit of a bender the first night. I came home the next day, Mark stayed with John for another day because he was still hungover and didn't want to drive. After Mark went home he rang me – it sounded like he was hallucinating. We didn't want some blabbermouth at a hospital ringing the press to say that Mark Preston had OD'd, so I scooped him up.'

'And what was really wrong?' Helen asked, still pissed at the fact that nobody had enlisted her help.

Andy looked away and shrugged.

'Kidney infection, bad one. We were wrong, Katie was right, he should have been in hospital. We got him to A&E as soon as we were sure nobody had spiked him, and they put him on painkillers and antibiotics. He'll be fine, but he's pissed off and he won't admit to Katie that he should have listened to her. He'll go home when he's calmed down. Who knew that a kidney infection would make you hallucinate?'

Helen nodded, still angry at being kept out of the loop. 'I've got stuff to do,' she said, and left.

'Let's go for a walk,' Andy said, putting his arm around Xan.

'Walkies?' Xan joked nervously.

'You got it, hon,' Andy said, hugging him.

They made their way down to the lake and walked along the shoreline to the limit of Xan's property. A small boat was tethered at the end of a short pier, and Andy rowed them out. The lapping of the waves and the sound of the wind in the trees was enough to drown out their voices from anyone on the shore. It was freezing on the water, and Xan shivered, despite the coat he'd put on as he left the house. Andy took off his own coat and wrapped it around Xan. Since the wolf infection, Andy didn't seem to feel the cold.

'What really happened?' Xan asked. 'Will you be ill too?'

Andy stared out across the water. 'I've got permission to tell you this,' he said carefully.

Xan's heart clenched; something had been kept from him? Mark had promised him that he wouldn't be kept out of the wolf club. He thought his scars entitled him to know what was happening.

Andy saw Xan flinch and understood. 'Nobody's lied to you. This is new. We took John's car and went out for a run, after you left with Helen. I split off from John and Mark, I wanted to try some new shapes and it seemed wise to be alone. I picked up a trace of a scent on the breeze. I assumed it was a dog, but it wasn't.'

'Another werewolf?' Xan spoke reverently.

'Yes, a woman. I'd ignored it, idiot that I am, but she managed to track us down and was waiting for John and Mark at the car. I panicked her a bit, there was a bit of an incident, but we all calmed down eventually and she took us back to where she lives.'

'Trusting of her,' Xan managed to say, knowing with a lover's heart what was coming.

'Very. I thought at first she wasn't long out of her teens, but it's the wolfie trait – you know that

Mark and John don't look their age – she looks about twenty, but she's only a couple of years younger than us. She's twenty-eight, end of this month.'

'And how does this affect Mark?' Xan asked slowly.

Andy closed his eyes. 'It's a fucking disaster. She knows who we are – she's not quite a fan, but she has all our albums, can you believe it? She's not interested enough in us to follow the gossip, and hadn't caught up with the fact that Mark has a girlfriend. She invited him into her house: object obvious. John and I left them to it.'

'Mark fucked this girl?' Xan was appalled. 'After everything he's said about leaving the fans alone? After all the crap he went through saving himself for Katie?'

'She's not a kid, and he wasn't saving himself for Katie, was he? He was saving himself for a wolfie woman, he just didn't wait long enough. This is so fucked up.' Andy closed his eyes. 'Mark said that he couldn't tear himself away from her, which sounded like he was infatuated – he's never done this before, remember? He's never met someone he couldn't keep his hands off. Well, we guessed that was all it was. Eventually his guilt dragged him away from Diana, and he went back to Katie.'

'Diana?' Xan took a deep breath. Just months ago, Mark was single and ripe for conquest, now the sneaky little git had two women. Xan would be having words with him, the first one being 'hypocritical'.

'Yeah, that's her name. I've not got an angle on her yet, we've not really seen her in any normal context. She's a researcher, same as Helen. Freakily similar to Helen actually, she's a geneticist. Her age is a nice bonus – remember how Mark used to give us that "when we find her, she could be fifteen or fifty" line? She's a redhead, not bad-looking, but nothing you'd notice in a crowd. Nice tits.'

Xan raised his eyebrows. 'Nice tits? You meet a werewolf, and that's your take on it?' Xan wasn't fooled, Andy was badly shaken. This was a complication he hadn't truly believed would come around. Mark and John would be reacting differently; they'd always assumed that they weren't the only ones, and it was just a matter of finding others.

'Is she attached?' he asked, realising as he said it that he was looking for problems, looking out for his friends. He felt eerily adult; he'd always known it would come one day, and here it was, the situation that made him understand that he had people to care for.

Andy nodded. 'She is now. To Mark. I've been through the house and seen no sign of a bloke, not even an ex. I think there were other women there, relatively recently, but she said they'd been lodgers. It's a biggish house, three storeys, basement, mid terrace, big, walled back garden.' He took a deep breath. 'Trouble came almost as soon as Mark went back home. He rang me, said he was really ill. I rang John and told him, and John got anxious about Diana. John, by the way, is very anxious about Diana, if you get my meaning.'

'Shit. We don't need this,' Xan whispered.

'We're stuck with it. John went to see her, found her exhausted, crazy, in pain. He tried to help her, but she wouldn't let him touch her, she was screaming for Mark. That's when we realised we were dealing with something a bit more drastic than infatuation. They're addicted to each other. I don't know for how long, or why, or how, but it's flaming obvious.' Andy sighed. 'And John's got that look about him, y'know? The White Knight look.'

'Yeah, he likes saving fair maidens, we know that. Does she want to be saved?'

Andy spoke carefully. 'She's barely noticed that he exists, but he's dealing with that pretty well, considering that we assumed he'd be Mr Werewolf if we ever found Mrs Werewolf. He says that she just wants to talk about Mark. John's interest in this woman is not a problem – he's dealing with it, believe it or not. To be honest, I think it's the wolf woman aspect that fascinates him, which isn't unexpected. The problem is that we've got someone who knows who we are, and that we're werewolves. She calls us Shifters, by the way, and seems to know a fuck of a lot about it. We have to keep her happy, and that means making sure that Mark doesn't piss her off. Which he will, because he's told me that he's made a commitment to Katie and he's not going to let her down.'

'Fuck,' Xan breathed. 'Will she keep quiet about us?' He blinked. 'I mean, you?'

'Us.' Andy bit his lip. 'It should be "us", I wish it was. Anyway, we spoke to her, we told her that someone else knows about us, and she agreed that you and she should meet. Like I said, she knows the Hearts. So, when are you free?'

Xan shrugged. 'Whenever. Where do you fit in?'

'Oh god. I told her that I was spoken for, and she didn't push it, but I get the feeling that I'm not off the hook.'

'Do you want to be?' Xan asked, truly jealous now.

'Let's deal with this a step at a time, eh? I'm yours, always, you know that?'

Xan smiled, his face pale in the bleak light of a December morning, and took the oars. 'I'll have to lie to Helen about this. I'll have to cover for you guys.'

'I know. It's bad enough that *I'm* lying to her…'

'I'll back you up,' Xan said. It was an extension of the old cover-up, after all.

Andy nodded and glanced at his watch. 'I'm going back, they won't have noticed yet that I'm not around. John's standing guard. I'll call you with the address later today, OK?'

'You don't know it?'

Andy shrugged. 'I could find the house blindfold from halfway across the world, I just don't know the street name or the house number.' He stood up, steady as a rock, and jumped to the pier, reaching out to steady the boat while Xan got out.

'I've got to go, I'm needed. I'll call you later.'

Xan watched him go, then went to his living room and found the tapes of the earliest sessions, John's voice higher, less controlled, even Mark making an occasional mistake, laughter, jokes, Helen's voice in the background, before it all got so complicated. He closed his eyes.

The phone call didn't come, and Xan tried Andy's phone twice. Nobody picked up. Next he tried Mark, who answered, and Xan heard a woman laughing in the background. He closed his eyes; he was being shut out again.

'Yo, Xan. Come over, we've been hoping you'd ring. Andy forgot to charge his phone, and me and John haven't got your new number with us.'

'You know my home number,' Xan whispered. There was a pause, then Mark said, 'Look, I'm sorry, we do want you here. We got carried away, talking.' Mark gave him the address and Xan headed to Manchester. He spotted Andy's car a few streets away, and didn't see John's at all. They were already being careful, protecting this woman. Xan would have to do the same. He parked a mile away, and thanked the winter cold that he could put on a cagoule and fleece and walk unrecognised.

John opened the door at the first knock; he already looked at home. He was stood in a narrow porch with doors that led to the living room and a hallway. Xan stepped into the living room and looked around, getting a first impression before too much happened. It was decorated in mature-student chic, which translated as cheap, cheerful and untidy. She had a decent sound system, and Xan gave her extra points for that. It was pretty new too – the CD player had only been on the market for three months, so it wasn't a leftover from a previous lover, if Andy was right about the lack of signs of male presence in the house. The house was clean with no artificial smells, just like John's flat. There were plenty of books and science journals, and not just biology – she read widely. She had a bookshelf full of science fiction, horror, fantasy. Some folklore books and a big Monet print Blu-tacked to the wall. He decided he could find nothing to object to and finally looked at the woman who was causing so much trouble.

God, her eyes. He was caught in them: wide green pools that pinned him down and inspected him. He was on trial here, he understood. She lowered her eyes, mock demure, and offered him a drink.

She was sharing a sofa with Mark, who was silent, watchful, his hand on her thigh in a possessive gesture. Mark looked shockingly thin and Xan noticed that Diana appeared tired and starved too. As she stood up to make drinks, Mark pulled her back down towards him and kissed her. They had such hunger for each other. Xan looked away; it was indecent for anyone else to be in the room with them.

John stood up. 'I'll make something to eat,' he said.

'We just ate,' Mark said, pushing Diana's hair

away from her face and touching the corner of her mouth, uplifted by her smile.

'You'll eat again,' John replied, a firmness in his voice that Xan had rarely heard him use with Mark.

Mark nodded. 'John, she's tired, will you make us a drink too?'

'I know where to find the teabags,' John said, not even trying to disguise the affection in his voice.

Xan watched all this and glanced at Andy who nodded, understanding that the whole dynamic of their little group had changed completely. Katie's arrival had barely dented the relationship between the five of them, but this woman could blow them apart. And she was a werewolf, a Shifter.

He kept his silence, watching her, trying to work things out. He was out of the wolf club, for now. He was outside the Ransome marriage too, he'd have to accept that, and he was already beginning to suspect that other things were changing, that Andy and Helen shared too much now and were leaving him behind. He only had the Hearts, and this woman might destroy the band – deliberately or not. If she took Mark's time and energy, and John's concentration, the band was dead in the water. If she took a dislike to any of the band, how much would years of friendship and loyalty count against the favours of the only female werewolf they'd ever met? Even Andy had expressed some sexual interest in her, and he'd not taken a second look at another woman since Helen agreed to marry him.

He heard Helen's voice, in his head, teasing. *Xan, put a positive light on it for once, will ya?* OK, he would. How could this be good for him? Firstly, obviously, she might be able to infect him. Secondly, all three of his closest male friends were already drawn to her, so she would hold them together, if things were handled right. Thirdly, she distracted Mark from Katie, who was already suspected of wanting the Hearts to call it a day and retire on their royalties. Fourthly, she was obviously firmly within the inner circle already, and he could share his secrets with her. Keeping his gob shut wasn't the easiest thing in the world for him.

However he looked at it, he couldn't afford to alienate her. He glanced at her again and was surprised to see that she was looking at him, obviously anxious. He smiled, hoping to reassure her. How many people knew her secret? She'd trusted him without even meeting him, putting her faith in whatever Mark had said about him. Xan swallowed, realising how much that meant to him.

She was talking to him but he was still lost in thought. He shook his head and apologised. She wanted to know about the biting, which shocked him at first, but he decided he liked her directness. He showed her his scars and she tore herself away from Mark for long enough to tell Xan that she held out little hope that a bite from her would have a different result, going so far as to advise him to stop torturing himself and them, and accept the way things were. She was clear that she wouldn't get involved. He knew her type – rampant pragmatists – this is how it is, make the best of it. She had no romance in her soul and would never strive for more.

She'd fight for what she had, though, he had no doubt of that, and the way she looked at Mark made it clear that she was fascinated by the Hearts' skinny guitarist. Andy, Mark and John joked about it, nervously: why had she chosen Mark when John had made a play?

John was an unexpectedly good loser. 'She'll have her reasons, even if she's not sure what they are right now. Anyway, it's not over until we're all dead and gone, is it? She might see sense yet.'

He'd wanted to stay, to spend time with her, to make sure that she knew how important all of this was for him, but Mark sent him away to lie for him.

Finally alone again, Diana led Mark back to her bed. He was apologetic at first, almost embarrassed by his need for her, but the wild magic lit up between them and they fell once more into a desperate tangle. They were both sore and exhausted, but their addiction gave them no mercy until finally, exhaustion took them and they sank into a restless sleep. When dawn came, they kissed again, gently, wary of bruised limbs and chafed skin. Tired caresses and soft words kept them together for an hour, as they slowly realised that the storm had spent itself. Diana left the bed and showered, coming back dressed.

'I think, maybe, you can leave now.' She spoke quietly, regretfully, and turned away as Mark made his way to the bathroom.

'I have to go,' he said, when she offered breakfast, and she didn't argue. There was nothing in his eyes for her, just confusion and guilt. He rang his cousin, who drove round to pick him up. With John waiting in the car, Mark gave Diana a hesitant hug, a dry kiss.

'Look, you can't talk about this…' he said.

Diana was amused – did he think she couldn't keep a secret?

'So I can't ring the tabloids?' she shot back.

He smiled a little. 'OK, I'm sorry. I … I just feel like you're getting a crap deal here.'

'I don't see it like that,' she told him. 'I do have a life, a job. Don't start feeling sorry for me.'

He kissed her again, dry lips on dry lips, quick, perfunctory; then opened the door and left.

Sane again, Diana turned on TV and checked Teletext. She didn't even know what day it was and realised she'd missed several days of work without even checking in. She went to work, hoping against hope that someone had done the basic maintenance work on her official experiments.

Chapter 22

A week later Diana summoned Xan to the house, took blood and skin samples, and dismissed him. She had seemed distant, and briefly mentioned that Mark had told her that he wasn't going to leave Katie.

He waited for another summons, and spent time with the band, but it felt like they'd all decided that 'the Diana thing' was a problem they had to solve before they saw her again. John was as unhappy as Diana had seemed to be, and Mark was blatantly lying to himself.

Xan knew better than anyone that the clock couldn't be turned back; trying to make things work as a trio with Helen and Andy had shipwrecked their relationships. They all wanted to rebuild things but Xan understood that the love affair was over, and he wasn't as important to either of them as they were to each other. On the surface nothing had changed; they still spent time with him and assured him that they loved him, but he could tell. They were nest-building, the bastards.

He sat in his kitchen, the pathetic daylight of a Lancashire January barely leaking through the window, feeling friendless and alone and thinking about how things were falling apart. The three werewolves talked only about Diana.

Mark seemed bewildered, and while his early wild addiction had gone, he admitted to feeling a growing compulsion to go back to her, and feared that giving her up wouldn't be easy. He'd said to the

rest of the Hearts that perhaps she would be better off with John. John had taken that as a green light from Mark, but after being rebuffed once was nervous about approaching her.
Diana must feel so isolated. Xan thought back to the way she'd been back in December: happy, laughing, trusting, a part of them. They had given her a taste of a family, then abandoned her and left her to rot.

He grabbed his car keys and went to her. The house was dark and closed up when he got there, and he wondered if he should have called first. He waited, walking up and down the street, before he realised that she would be at work.

She got home at seven, snow in her hair as she walked down the street, clearly in a world of her own. She let herself in, the light went on and she was silhouetted against the window for a few seconds as she drew the thick curtains together. Light spilled from the transom window above the door. He drew his breath and knocked. She recognised him, even wrapped up against the chill, and stood aside silently to let him in.

He hadn't meant to descend immediately into self-pity; he'd intended to sound like he was boldly grasping the nettle when he asked her to confirm that the infection would never take. He ended up whining – he knew it – and he knew she was impatient with him. She explained things but he'd never been much interested in science, and it washed over him. All he knew was that he was denied forever what he wanted so much.

He begged for friendship then, a place in her world. He knew that she was beyond puzzled by him; why on earth should he need her friendship? She was wary and distant, and definitely wanted him out of the way so she could get back into her routine.

He found an angle, asking her about her financial security, asking how she was coping now that her lodgers were gone – it must be hard on her, struggling alone. She denied it, telling him the house was hers, free and clear, she had money coming in, she was earning. Ah, but Xan had an idea of how research got done: pay the young scientists a pittance and keep them on short contracts without benefits. A couple of weeks ago, before they'd stopped talking about it, Mark had wondered openly if Diana would be willing to have kids. Now that the guys had found a woman like them, it was a subject on their minds: would the trait breed true?

Xan worked on that angle, asking Diana how she'd cope if she couldn't work, if she had kids one day. Just a flicker of fear in her eyes, fear of a secret broken too early, and he stopped cold. It had already happened.

No, Mark didn't know. Yes, of course Mark was the father. And no, Andy and John didn't know either, and Diana would be very grateful if Xan kept his big gob shut.

And yes, if he wanted to stay there was a spare room and he was welcome to it. She understood, in the end, that he was there because he was lonely, and thought that she might be too.

But he was Xan, and she was young, and vaguely pretty, and not even the fear of Mark's fury and the demise of the Hearts could keep Xan from trying. He knew it was crazy, and he suspected he was being the biggest bastard of all time, but he slipped into her bed, spinning a tale about nightmares and not being able to sleep alone. And she cuddled him, and told him to sleep, and was totally, undeniably unresponsive to his presence: he might as well have been a stuffed toy. He went to sleep surprisingly quickly, the phrase 'this has never happened to me before' echoing in his mind.

He woke up with an erection, wide-eyed, suddenly and completely certain that Mark and John knew what he'd tried to do, and were on their way to Diana's, planning to kill him. The only question was whether they'd do it slowly or quickly. She was gone from the bed. She'd probably only slept a couple of hours. He showered quickly and nervously headed downstairs. He found a key on the table downstairs, with a note: 'Help yourself to breakfast, feel free to visit anytime.'

That was it, the moment when he looked inside himself and saw only the brat prince, the spoiled and needy boy who floated through life because he was beautiful and talented, and because four good people tolerated him and saw something good in him. Five good people, now.

Chapter 23

Diana was pregnant with Mark's child and keeping it secret, not asking for help, dealing with it in her own way. Each time Xan looked at her, he saw someone who was confident and self-assured. Scant months earlier, he would have seen a rival, an enemy. Now he saw a friend and an ally.

He was gradually moving into Diana's place, finding it homely and comfortable. Helen and Andy protested that he wasn't around much, but he told himself they weren't protesting hard enough – they seemed almost relieved. It wasn't over, and he was still Helen's lover, still Andy's lover, but they weren't the heart of his world any more.

Diana's body changed, he saw it and loved it. He'd never been around a pregnant woman before, and he delighted in the development of her body shape. He found out what she wanted from him: someone to talk to, someone to cuddle up to and watch stupid films with, someone to listen to new music with and pick it apart. She loved it when he played it camp, when he dressed up and strutted around the house; he was her clown and happy to be so.

Mark visited and didn't notice that she was pregnant. It was always a flying visit: he'd arrive furious, angry with the addiction that forced him there, and he left reluctantly, appeased, reminded that Diana was a friend, not a threat. Xan was appalled by Mark's behaviour, which would leave Diana bruised and scratched. Diana assured him that Mark didn't leave unscathed.

Andy dropped by once, puzzled by Xan's presence, and slightly hurt by it. Diana explained calmly that they were friends, no more, and Andy accepted it. Andy sent presents, something else that Diana found hilarious, and also vaguely insulting. Expensive teas, rare coffee blends, fine wines, treats from the deli. Andy was trying to educate Diana, and she knew his game.

As for John, he was around a lot. He rarely asked to stay over, accepted Xan's role in Diana's life with equanimity, and seemed to be weighing the situation up. He treated Diana with affectionate, friendly respect, but did not push things further. Diana would go out running as a wolf with Mark, or John, or both of them. John found out that Xan was sleeping in Diana's bed, and seemed to believe that it was platonic, a comfort thing. He'd looked at Xan, weighing things up.

'The first time you got in that bed, that wasn't the plan, was it?' His tone had been even.

'Possibly not. I don't remember,' Xan hedged.

'You're not her type,' John said, quietly. It was possibly the cruellest thing he'd ever said to Xan, but Xan knew that he deserved it and swallowed it down. He considered retaliation but realised he'd grown beyond that. John waited for the barb to fly, and seemed surprised when Xan kept his silence.

John's visits were usually quite short; he lived relatively close by and had developed a habit of dropping in a couple of times a week, just for an hour or so. Diana had given up on treating him as a guest and instead carefully made space for him.

One evening, as the front door slammed shut behind the departing singer, Diana took the chair opposite the TV and sipped her tea.

'Xan?'

'Hmmm?' He was reading a book of ghost stories.

'Xan.' Her voice was sharper, and he looked up.

'Sorry. Got absorbed by this story. What's up?'

'Why is John around here so much?' There was a hesitation in her voice that hit him in the stomach.

'Um, maybe he's making sure that he's allowed to be?'

'What about Andy?'

'Andy won't visit you here without an invitation. It's not that he doesn't like you, but he appreciates you want your privacy and thinks it's too risky, being spotted in this part of town, where he has no reason to be. He's pretty distinctive, and he's married.'

'Oh.' Diana shrugged. 'It doesn't bother you.'

'Hon, I go out in disguise.' He smiled, watching her. He did: he combed his hair flat, put on some specs, took off the make-up and wore geeky clothes. Nobody looked at him twice. He realised that it didn't matter to her; she saw the same person however glammed up. 'John's most distinctive features are his hair and eyes. He always turns up wearing shades with his hair tied back, and he wears baggy clothes too. Mark turns up in a bloody duffle coat! We're taking care not to bring any gossip to your door.'

'OK.' She nodded. 'That's a good idea. It's my natural instinct, you know? To hide my association with them. With you. I've been thinking, it's actually good that Mark has a girlfriend. So long as he's publicly associated with her, she's shielding me and my baby from attention. She's no threat to me, because Mark obviously loves her and wants to stay with her, so he won't tell her about me. And Mark can't leave me, can he? We're addicted to each other.'

This was Xan's role, her spy within the band.

'It looks like it. Don't put yourself down, though, he does like you.'

'I wish he'd show it,' she said, then looked down, obviously scared that she'd said too much.

'Wolf girl, hush. He doesn't do that, he's not affectionate like that. I know it's not easy for you, but at least you have more from him than…' He stopped.

'More than what?' She looked up. 'More than who?' She looked at him, understanding dawning. 'Oh, Xan. I'm sorry,' she whispered. 'I didn't know.'

'You and him are about the only ones who don't. I've given up, he's obviously never going to be interested in me as anything other than a friend.'

She smiled sadly. 'I'd like him to see me as a friend instead of as a problem. He's so hung up about being unfaithful to Katie that he barely speaks to me these days. It's like he thinks if he doesn't talk when he's with me, it doesn't count.'

Xan closed his eyes; it was unbearable to him that Mark could be so shitty.

'Ah well, at least he talks to me. Between us we have a great relationship with him.' Xan managed a smile. 'It's a shame we can't swap places sometime, you could get to talk all night with him and I'd get my dirty little paws on him.'

Diana looked up, her eyes full of mischief. 'You could hide in my bed next time he visits. He's so eager to slake his addiction he might not even notice it's you at first.'

'Jesus.' Xan closed his eyes. 'Thank you for that thought. I'll treasure it.' He smiled in turn. 'But I can't work out a way to give you the night of conversation. If I could, I would.'

She was smiling at him and he raised his eyebrows. 'Talk to me, girlfriend. I know you want to,' he teased.

'Hasn't he got the most beautiful hands?' she said, blushing. It was clear that she'd never indulged in a conversation like this.

'Don't get me started. I could watch him play guitar forever. I dream of the things that those hands could do to me.'

'And his hair. I love the way he glories in it. It's the only thing he's vain about. Him and John and Andy, they all think they've got the best hair!'

'And who has?' Xan teased.

She blushed again. 'Mark, of course. Sometimes I can almost see reflections in it.'

'Ooh, what sort of reflections?' Xan opened his eyes very wide, and was gratified by the way she shut up instantly, embarrassed half to death.

She stood up. 'Tea? Coffee? Beer?' she asked.

'Beer. Is it OK if I stay tonight?'

She nodded. He always asked, despite the fact that one of the spare bedrooms was now emphatically his, and he was paying rent to her.

He called her back. 'Di?'

She turned around.

'Tomorrow's Saturday. Do you fancy a drive up to my place? I need to check it out, make sure it's OK, and I want to see Helen and Andy. If you want, I could say that you're my girlfriend, and you could meet Helen. I know you'll like her.'

She considered it then nodded. 'Yes, I'll go up to the house with you, I'll follow in my car. I've got to nip into the lab first thing and then I'm all yours. But no, I don't want to meet Helen. I think this low-profile thing is for the best. Is there somewhere I could lurk if she comes round when I'm there?'

Xan was insulted. 'I'm not going to hide you away!'

'Then you'll have to make sure I get a bit of warning so I can leave quickly,' Diana said firmly. 'I don't want to meet her.'

Xan put on his most miserable face. 'OK,

I'll leave you at my place to explore and I'll go to the Ransomes' alone. I just want you two to be friends,' he said.

'Want away,' Diana said, not unkindly. 'I can't see how it can happen. Unless somehow you puzzle out a way to convey to her that me being a werewolf and wanting to jump her husband isn't necessarily a threat to her.' She opened her eyes comically wide. 'Oops,' she said, that mischief in her eyes again.

He couldn't help it, he laughed. 'You think I didn't know about that? Watch it, sister, Andy's *my* boyfriend.'

'Yeah, you want mine, I want yours.' She flashed a quick smile at him, and danced into the kitchen.

Damn right I want yours, he thought. She was so bloody cute like this: relaxed, at ease with him. He'd sleep in his own bed tonight – it seemed like the safest option.

They drove up to the lakeside house. Diana refused to drive at his pace so he had to stop and draw a map for her. She arrived twenty minutes behind him, curious about his home. She loved it immediately; it offered privacy and space, and was emphatically a bachelor pad. He was already surveying the living room and the hi-fi system with some alarm.

'I'll have to move some of this stuff if you're going to bring the baby here,' he said.

She shrugged; she didn't seem to be thinking

ahead to the baby stage, and was still avoiding the fact that she hadn't told Mark about the pregnancy. He would notice her shape soon. Xan was feeling utterly frustrated by her intransigence, but it was out of his hands. He watched as she explored the ground floor of the house, delighted by the state-of-the-art PC, the racks of videos, vinyl, CDs and books, and the semi-professional music studio at the back of the house.

'Do you record here?' she asked, fascinated, going completely fangirl on him.

'God, no, it's pretty basic stuff here. We use this place for writing and early rehearsals, and when we decide that we know what we're doing we go to a proper studio. Do you want to try the drums?'

'I'd break something,' she said, suddenly shy.

'Oh, come on, you wouldn't.'

She shrugged. 'Xan, you don't know me. I'd break something.' She had that stubborn look again. She didn't want to trespass here – this was Hearts business. He didn't push it.

'OK, then. I told Hel that I'd be there for a late lunch. Andy knows that you're here, I didn't get round to mentioning it to the others. Did you?'

'If they go to my house assuming I'll be there, that's their problem,' she said calmly. 'Besides, they both have keys; they can let themselves in and strip-mine the fridge whether I'm there or not.'

'Yeah, fridge.' He checked the contents and pulled milk out of the freezer, along with a couple of loaves of bread and a large pack of crumpets. He looked in the salad compartment and shuddered.

Diana glanced towards the fridge. 'Xan, go and see Helen. I'll sort out your experiments in home composting.'

'Ta, hon. It's good to have a woman around,' he teased. She didn't rise to the bait.

'Is there anywhere I can't go?' she asked.

'Nowhere, my home is your home,' he said. 'I'll see you later.'

When he got back home, John was there and Diana wasn't. A large bouquet of roses was scattered on the floor. There was a fresh red splash of blood pooling next to them and John looked shaken. He had a tea towel wrapped around his arm.

Xan glanced around, understanding the situation immediately.

'What happened?' he asked quietly, ominously. 'Where's the girl?'

'She drove off,' John said. 'I've only been here for ten minutes. Bloody redheads, she's got a real temper on her.'

'Did you touch her?'

'No. Yes. No. Jesus. I heard that you were here for the weekend, and thought she might be lonely, so I went to her place. She wasn't there, just a note for Mark saying that she was here, so I rang Mark in case he needed to know and came here to see her.'

'Armed with two dozen red roses? You'd decided it was time to make a move?' Xan was surprised by how dangerous he sounded.

'Xan, she's not your girlfriend, she's a free agent.'

'She's my friend, and I won't have you treating her like—'

'Like you and me treat every other lass we meet? OK, fair enough, I know this isn't something I can walk away from next month. That's why I've not done anything before. Xan, I like her.'

'She deserves better than "like".'

'She expects better than that.' John sat down and closed his eyes. 'Xan, help me. I've never done this before.'

Xan laughed.

'Seriously, I've not. Hell, how often do I have to do the chasing? And even when I do need to make an effort, it's usually just a game. And if they're really not interested, I can smile politely, admit I made a mistake, and chalk it up to experience. I can't do that with Diana. I have to be with her.'

'Why?'

'Because she haunts my dreams,' John said. 'She's already admitted that we'll be together one day, but she won't give me a clue when.'

'Why's she run away?' Xan was still worried.

'I fucked up. I tried the cocky rock-star act, I thought she'd like it. I walked in, saw that she was alone, grabbed her and told her that I wanted her. She damn near broke my arm getting free, said that I wanted the wolf woman, and that if and when I ever wanted Diana Foster, I should try again. Then she grabbed her keys – that's when she knocked the roses on the floor – and ran off.'

'Is she upset?' Xan asked.

'I'd say so. Yes. I'm so sorry.' John was getting over the shock now, and was genuinely stricken. He unwrapped the tea towel and peered at his bloody arm. 'Fuck, have you got any bandages? I heal fast, but I'm bleeding a storm here, I think she got an artery.'

'She hurt you?'

'Claws from nowhere, that's how she got away from me so fast.' He was almost in tears. 'I've never forced myself on anyone, she didn't have to do that, she could just have asked me to let go.'

Xan shook his head. 'She told me that the bond with Mark started with the first kiss. All she had to go on was your reputation and your clear intentions. If she'd kissed you, she might have been committed to more than she wants right now. She's got a lot on her mind.'

'Like what?' John asked, genuinely curious.

Xan stopped himself just in time, it really wouldn't be right for John to know about the baby before Mark did. 'Oh, work stuff, house stuff, fretting about Mark and Katie. Give her some space.' He got bandages from the bathroom and clumsily bound John's wound. 'Do you want to go to the hospital?'

'God, no. I'm shaking, I could do with a cuppa…'

Xan stared at him, his expression bleak. 'Make it yourself. I'm going back to Manchester. Use your keys to lock up.'

He caught up with Diana's car just outside Manchester, flashing his lights at her. She pulled over on the hard shoulder and he followed suit. She ran to his window and leaned in.

'Xan. You're looking very pretty, and it's broad daylight.'

He glanced in his mirror and nodded. She had a cooler head than him. He was appropriately geekish when they finally got back to her place. She was all smiles, and started to put a meal together.

'Well, that visit was a success,' she remarked casually, calling through from the kitchen. 'John popped by, did you catch him?'

'Yeah, he told me you weren't too pleased to see him.'

She peered through the doorway. 'He was very pleased to see me, alone,' she said. 'Did you set me up, Xan?'

Her tone was calm; she might as well have been asking if he wanted chips or mash with his sausages. He felt cold.

'No. I didn't. And I don't appreciate that kind of accusation.' Oh great, now they were arguing.

'I don't appreciate having to defend myself against John Preston.' She glowered.

'If you'd told him to stop it, he would have.'

'In the heat of the moment I didn't want to risk him not stopping. But OK–' she nodded – 'if you say you didn't set me up, I believe you. Chips or mash?'

And there, she'd closed off completely. Xan

wasn't having that – this needed to be sorted.

'Chips.' He went into the kitchen to chip the spuds she'd peeled. 'Don't you fancy him at all?' he asked.

'He's beautiful,' she said. 'He's also an arrogant sexist pig with no manners.'

'What makes you say that?' Xan asked, shocked. Of all the men he knew, he believed that John was the most naturally feminist.

'He just grabbed me! He wants the wolf woman, and he thinks he's entitled.' Now her voice was trembling. 'He's not, and he can't. I deserve more than that.'

'Honey?' Oh, and now she was pressed against him, crying against his chest. This was new. He could deal with this, and he hugged her. He turned off the heat under the chip pan and led her to the sofa. 'Come on, sweetheart, let it out.'

'I want them to see *me*, not just the wolf,' she said eventually, between sobs. 'Shit, I'm sorry, I shouldn't be laying this on you. It's just that I never expected to meet them, then when I did, they made me think that I was a part of something, and now I hardly see them. I hate this, I wish I'd never met them.'

'Oh honey…'

She looked up, defiant. 'You're the only good thing to come out of all this. You're the best friend I've ever had, and I feel guilty about that too because I'm keeping you away from being Xan Kendrick, aren't I? I know you must be bored, hanging around here.'

'I was getting bored with being Xan Kendrick anyway. Maybe it's time to grow up. Diana, I love you to bits, you know that?'

'Yeah, same goes. Why couldn't you have been a Shifter too? I could have wanted you then, and this would be so much easier.'

He smiled wryly, but she didn't see it. She loved him as a friend. That was OK, he could live with that, and it was best not to add to her troubles by trying to spell out to her every different way in which he loved her. It was hard to remember that he'd only known her for a few weeks. Besides, he was old enough to recognise that these feelings of his might just be a daft crush because she was Mark's lover and the closest thing he had to Mark.

'John and Andy fancy non-Shifters, and even Mark gave in eventually,' he pointed out, gently.

'Andy's made, not born, and not everyone's the same anyway. I never wanted anyone until I saw Mark.'

'Yeah? And look how he treats you.' Xan couldn't help it; Mark was pissing him off.

She swallowed hard and wiped her eyes. 'Yeah, but that's Mark, it's different. I won't put up with it from John.'

They ate, and then she sent him away, knowing that he'd made plans to spend time with Andy that evening. She would be fine, she told him.

John was still at the house, sitting on the pier in the dark, staring out at the lake. He made room for Xan.

'Is she OK?'

'She's a sensible lass,' Xan said.

'Sensible enough to send thee and me packing anyway,' John said, managing a smile. 'I'm going to have to apologise to her. I misread her.'

'No, she wants you, but she doesn't believe that you're interested in her. She thinks you want the wolf woman.'

'She is the wolf woman,' John said, picking up a stray pebble and skipping it across the water. 'But yeah, I know what you mean. I'm gonna have to go courting, aren't I?' He smiled, looking almost happy at the prospect. 'Any hints?'

Xan lay his head on John's shoulder, friend to friend. 'She'd kill me if she thought I was giving you clues. Work it out yourself, eh?'

They sat in silence until the moon rose, and then made their way back to the house.

That Sunday night, Diana's phone rang. She spoke into it for a while, glancing at Xan, her voice level, and then sat down and turned on the TV, flicking through the channels aimlessly.

'Who was that.'

'Arrogant sexist pig,' she said.

'And what did he want?'

'He wanted to take me out for a meal, then to a party. Is he mad?'

Xan considered. 'It might be OK, you know? If it's just once or twice, you might get away with it. People only talk about John's girlfriends when it lasts more than a month.'

'I said no,' she said emphatically. 'And he'll

be here straight away. He says. Pig.'

'Betcha wish you hadn't given him that key now.' Xan teased.

'I'll change the locks.' She looked at him and smiled. 'But you, you can have a key. Mark can go whistle.'

'Damn right you'll give me a key, I pay rent!'

'That ain't rent, it's protection money. I guard your skinny ass from all those mad groupies.'

There was a knock at the door.

'Enter, pig,' Xan called out.

John opened the door and looked round.

'Where did you call from?' Xan asked.

'Next street. Diana, please? I'm sorry, I was out of order. Don't sulk at me.'

'I'm not sulking. I don't sulk. Not even when people accuse me of sulking,' Diana said evenly. 'Apology accepted. How's the arm?'

'Scabby,' John said. 'But I'll live. Sorry again.'

'If I'd wanted to kill you, you'd know about it,' she said.

'Or not,' Xan joked, then shrugged and hid behind a newspaper. 'Ignore me,' he said.

'Can we talk?' John asked.

'Sure we can,' Xan said.

John took a deep breath. 'Diana, can *we* talk? In private?'

'No,' she said.

'OK, it won't be the first time I've made an idiot of myself in front of Xan. Diana, I've thought about it, and it's obvious that what we all have together isn't a temporary thing. You and Mark belong together, and the rest of us come as a package with Mark.'

'A pack,' Diana said, half-smiling.

'Yeah, if you like.' John took the seat next to Xan on the sofa. 'Not only that, but you've given hints that you'd like to have me and Andy as your lovers too. One day.'

'She can fuck off,' Xan muttered. 'He's mine.'

John reached out and clamped his hand firmly over Xan's mouth and nostrils, watching as he went red, then purple before letting go.

'Whoops, I meant to just cover your mouth. I reckon I overestimated how fucking big it is. I wonder how that happened?'

Xan took a deep breath and kissed John on the forehead. 'I love it when you get masterful,' he managed to say eventually, and hid behind his newspaper again.

Diana was watching them, keeping her face straight. 'One day. Perhaps. No promises.'

'One day,' John repeated, and found his thread again. 'When that day comes, I want us to be friends. I want you to know that I care about you and respect you. I don't want you to have a bad opinion of me. If it works for us like it works for you and Mark, then it'll be forever, and forever deserves a good start, yeah?'

He had her attention now, and carried on. 'OK, we were doing well, getting on OK, until I screwed up. You know that I'm on your side, don't you?'

Diana nodded. 'I know that if I'm in danger or in trouble, you'll be there. It doesn't mean that you like me, though, it just means you're protecting your future.'

John blinked; this was evidently harder than he'd expected.

'Sure, I can see how you'd think that. But you've made the same mistake you accused me of. You're not trying to understand me, to get to know me. You know things about me and you make assumptions.'

'I do?'

'You see that I have lots of girlfriends and jump to the conclusion that I don't like women. That's just crazy. I love women. I love talking to women, I love working with women, we had a woman producer for our first two albums. That was my idea. I also happen to like fucking, it's the way I am. I'm blessed with a hell of a sex drive, and I don't see any reason to be ashamed of it. I don't have long-term girlfriends because I'm a werewolf and I'm a really bad liar. It wouldn't work. I treat my partners well, I always make sure that they come if they want to, and I always, always say thank you. If you think that there's something wrong about two consenting adults having fun together, that's your right, but I'm not a user. They all know the deal and I often end up with a new friend.'

Diana flushed. 'You're determined to put your case.'

'I am. I made a mistake with you. I thought you'd enjoy the way I came on to you. I was wrong.

I thought you'd over-reacted, but thinking about it, thinking about how quickly you and Mark became addicted to each other, maybe you were right.'

'I was,' she said.

John glanced at Xan who was very still, staring at the newspaper. He spoke again.

'Diana, I'm not much cop at speeches, but please, give me a chance. We know that we'll be lovers, and we both want things to be better than they are with you and Mark. I know you love him, but it's not ideal, is it? Here's the deal, I want you, and nothing on earth can change that. You've already got Mark, so you don't need me as much as I need you. That means that I have to try harder than you. I ain't used to that.'

'No, you're not. You're right, though.'

'I know.' John grinned. 'How about we try to be friends, we build something good, and when you're ready, we'll move on? If I do something wrong, you tell me.'

'Oh, she'll tell you,' Xan interrupted.

John ignored him. 'If I'm on the right track, give me some encouragement. And maybe we could hold off from drawing blood?'

Diana stood up. 'Maybe I did jump to conclusions. OK, we'll play it your way.'

'No, we'll play it your way,' John said. Xan noticed his relief. When he looked at Diana, he saw she was nervous as hell.

Chapter 24

Three in the living room. Not three in a bed, but Xan reflected it was nearly as much fun. Diana and John were definitely courting, and it delighted Xan to see how shy they were with each other. If he'd been the man he used to be, he would have teased John half to death. John had never, ever spent so much energy on impressing any woman. The guy was in love, and it was cute. And Diana was half horrified by John's attention, caught in a mindset where she had a boyfriend and was going to be faithful to him. The fact that her wonderful Mark was making wedding plans with another woman was neither here nor there to her. And yet she obviously cared about John and wasn't merely flattered by his attention as she grew to know him.

Xan watched with warm affection. He loved both of them and wished that they'd get on with it. He also wished that Mark would behave like a half-decent human being, and was relieved when Diana finally gave him permission to tell Mark the news about the pregnancy. The woman was too unsure of Mark's reaction to tell him herself, and that told Xan all he needed to know about the amount of support she expected. He suggested, cautiously, that she forget Mark and marry him. He hid it behind a joke, behind self-mockery, and was grateful he'd not tried to be serious when she shot him down in flames.

He went to Leeds, arriving past midnight. Katie was furious about being woken up, but Mark explained to her that it was the kind of thing that

Xan did, and that it was part of their friendship.

'This better be important,' he said, getting into the passenger seat of Xan's car, shutting the door and looking straight ahead.

'It doesn't get any more important. She's pregnant.'

Mark stopped breathing and Xan watched him carefully. He let his breath out and smiled, so quickly, so subtly, that Xan wondered if he'd imagined it.

'Take me to her,' Mark said. 'Now.'

'Yeth, Marthter,' Xan muttered.

This was one night when Xan wasn't going to stop over. He dropped Mark off, watching him stand awkwardly at the front door, gathering the courage to go in. He watched as Mark knocked several times before taking a key out of his wallet. Xan waited until the door swung open, and then drove away, back to the house he'd not seen for days.

It changed everything, Mark became contrite, guilty, and very attentive to Diana, who blossomed and gained a new confidence. She was the one who insisted that Mark's wedding to Katie go ahead, she was the one who explained that her instincts were to keep any link between her and the male werewolves a secret. John failed to understand, and took his turn to propose marriage to her. She was gentler with him than she'd been with Xan, but she still refused him. She was Mark's girl; her attitude was plain. It didn't stop her spending long minutes staring at John though, wistful and sweet.

She took to hanging out at Xan's place, more confident now about spending time with the men. She liked the lakeside house, and asked if she could deliver the babies there. She knew it was twins as there were too many kicks in too many places for any other explanation. She refused any medical help, confident that Mark would be able to cope.

Xan was frustrated, telling her that Mark was just a guy who played guitar, but Diana gave him that distant, stubborn 'I'm not listening' smile, and he gave up. Let her bleed to death; that would teach the daft bint. He panicked as things came to a head. Diana was due the same week that Mark and Katie were getting married. Xan talked to John and Andy and they agreed that Mark couldn't possibly go ahead with the wedding – they had to do something else. If Diana wanted privacy, they could give up the band, go and hide out somewhere, tell Helen, tell Auntie Fran, take them with them, maybe even try to infect Hel…

Xan plotted and schemed, and nothing that Diana said could soothe the panic in his heart.

Chapter 25

Diana enjoyed spending time at the lake house. She could relax away from neighbours and the busy streets. She loved the house, the big windows at the back, the pier with the rowing boat, the modern kitchen. It always felt like a holiday home. She was careful not to put her stamp on it in case Xan had unexpected visitors. She also started to travel there with Xan, leaving her car at home. It would avoid awkward questions if Helen ever visited unexpectedly and saw Diana's car.

When she moved in at the end of the pregnancy, she took the chance to go through her research notes. She'd taken cell samples regularly from all four of the men, and they confirmed what she already knew from her studies of female Shifters. The werewolf trait was due to an entire chromosome, which she'd named the 'W'. All the Shifters she'd tested had a pair of W chromosomes alongside the rest of their genome, and there was absolutely no variation in those chromosomes. They must have been self-repairing, with some underlying structure that either prevented or repaired any mutation. None of Xan's cells contained the chromosome, nor any immune response that Diana could track back to it. He'd said he'd been ill when the others tried to infect him, but it must have been a reaction to other pathogens. Andy's cells were a delight to study, especially on a monthly basis. He was a chimeric being, with most of his cells now positive for the W and some still without it. His proportion of W cells went up slightly as time went by.

Diana's sample size of Shifters was still very low: herself, Andy, Mark, John, her sister Joyce and her ex-housemates. Who she still hadn't mentioned to the guys. At first she'd kept quiet in case the men proved to be dangerous, and then she'd kept quiet because she didn't want Mark, John or Andy going off in search of the women who had failed to contact her over the last year. Something had happened to them, and Diana doubted it was anything good.

Her thoughts on the whereabouts of her sister led her to think about their mother. It had been a while since they'd spoken. Diana rang from a public phone in the nearest town and assured her that she was fine. Her mother asked if she had heard from Joyce, as it had been over a year since she'd had any news. She asked Diana if she'd like to come home for a few days. It had been a long time since she'd suggested a meeting, and Diana gladly accepted. Then she mentioned that she was pregnant.

Mrs Foster went very quiet and then asked Diana who the father was. Before she could reply, her mother asked her *what* the father was. Without naming any names, Diana explained about Mark, and Xan, and John and Andy. Her mother was furious, said that Diana was an idiot, that the men could not be trusted, and that Diana should pack her bags and go back to her. Diana hung up and walked back to the lake house. All four men were hanging around, drawn there by the impending birth.

Diana was upset, and Mark picked up on it. He wanted to meet Diana's mother and reassure her, but Diana talked him out of it. She told him that she'd wait until the babies were born and then take them to meet their grandmother. Diana had a few months of maternity leave before she went back to work, after all.

Mark stared at her. 'Back to work?' he said.

'Yeah. I mean, my house is paid for, but I can't live on fresh air, and I like my job.'

'Well, we'll have to find childcare … will the babies be OK? I mean, they won't Change, will they?'

'Did you?' she asked.

He shook his head. 'I think Mum would have mentioned it. OK. I need to divert money to you without Katie noticing. Shit.'

Andy looked up. 'I can sort that out. We'll set up an account for Diana, give it a vaguely business-y name, and pay it from the band account. We'll put her down as a consultant. I'll sort it out.' He nodded at her. 'If you ever need more, urgently, let me know and I'll sort it. Don't go to Mark – Katie already has him signed up to a joint account and she checks the statements. I know how to move money.'

Diana looked puzzled, so he went on to explain.

'I'm not just the bass player in the Hearts. Ever heard of Ransome Industries? I'm the sole heir, and I'm on the board now, have been since I turned twenty-five. Helen's independently wealthy too, and Xan. The band brings in good money, but the three of us have family money and my mum and dad have been training me to manage it and move it about since I was about twelve. The band self-manages; I forgot you wouldn't know. Look, we'll sort out an income for you, no problem, then you can go back to work because you want to, not because you have to.'

Mark scowled. 'I should pay.'

There was a short silence, and then Xan spoke up. 'No, this isn't just about you and Diana, there's something bigger going on. I'm happy to use band money for this. John?'

The older Preston cousin looked up. 'What? Look, if Andy says it's OK and you and Mark agree, it's fine by me.'

'Mark?' Xan asked.

This time Mark rolled his eyes. 'Fine.'

Chapter 26

As her time came closer, Diana's calm deepened, and a couple of weeks before the babies were due, she left work and moved into Xan's house. That meant keeping Helen away; a girl in Xan's house wouldn't be an issue, but a pregnant woman would be. Xan was saddened by how easy it seemed to be to distract Helen, who was busy helping Mark with his half of the wedding guest list. Mark's family consisted of John and Frances. He'd asked Fran and John to each invite some friends, and asked Andy's parents and Helen's mum along. After that, his allocation would be filled with friends from the business. Helen was busy ringing around, finding out who would actually be attending.

Xan and John tried to keep any hint of the wedding preparations away from Diana, but she brushed aside their protection. Mark was living a double life, even in his own mind. Away from the lake house, he talked about the wedding and spoke fondly of Katie and how happy they were. Inside the house he spent every minute he could with Diana, the pair of them sneaking away to make love whenever possible. Mark was a man divided, and Xan wondered how long he could bear it without going mad.

The babies arrived before the wedding: two crazily redheaded little boys, ugly as sin and twice as loud. With the exception of Diana, they were all instantly infatuated with them. Their mother regarded them with a mixture of puzzlement and scientific interest, as if she hadn't really expected to produce babies at all. Xan felt a proprietorial interest in the boys – he was the one living with Diana, after all – but suddenly the three Shifters were paying a hell of a lot of attention to Diana and 'their' babies. Xan realised, within hours of the birth, that all three of them were claiming a kind of paternity to the babies, based on their shared W chromosome. Sometimes it was hard to be the outsider.

Helen rang once, wondering what 'her boys' were up to, and warning Mark that Katie was on the verge of cancelling the wedding. Katie had told Helen that she could put up with an extended stag night, and that she'd expected it, but Mark had to switch his phone on and bloody well talk to her. Katie was a mess of nerves and needed to talk to her fiancé.

Xan had an instant of sympathy for Katie; she was going to get dumped at the altar, near enough, and that was going to be harsh. He was horrified when Mark went along with it, and preparations for the wedding continued at Diana's behest. He almost felt sorry for Katie now, seeing a ruthlessness in Diana that hadn't been obvious before. His own inherent streak of bitchiness, controlled and subdued over the last nine months, applauded the way that Diana had turned Mark's marriage to Katie into a victory for herself.

'She can have him because you say it's OK? Is that how it works?' he asked her, in a rare moment of privacy.

'I don't want her to have him. I want him with me, all day, all night. I want us to be together forever, with our sons and the next ones, and the ones after that. I can't have that, though, I have to hide, and I can't do that if I'm Mrs Mark Preston.'

'But it makes you feel better that she's got him because you said it was OK?'

She blinked. 'He loves her. He doesn't love me. I wouldn't encourage him to be with someone he didn't care about, that would be wrong.'

'But you'll force him to lie to someone he loves?' Xan couldn't let go of it, although he knew he was heading into trouble. 'Is that your way of getting back at him for claiming that he doesn't love you?'

'People see the same thing through different eyes. I feel no anger towards Katie. She's done me no wrong so why should I be vindictive towards her?'

'She doesn't even know you exist!'

'Exactly. She has Mark, I have the facts. I think it's a fair balance.'

He gave up.

The day before the wedding, they left her and the babies in the lakeside house. It all felt unreal. She and Mark had been joking with each other, and in front of Xan, it looked for the first time as if Mark and Diana were a real couple; they were giving each other such support, such strength, disguised as jokes and teasing. When it had become clear that the wedding wouldn't be cancelled, John had lost it and refused to stand as best man in what he saw as a betrayal of Diana. Andy and Xan knew better; they understood that Katie was the one betrayed, lied to on her wedding day. Andy had no compunction whatsoever about standing in for John. He was more than willing to lie to Katie because he'd found her attempts to interfere with band business so annoying.

The ceremony was in Mark's local church. Katie had wanted a church wedding, but had no particular affiliation to any. Frances had suggested a little chapel in a village near Ulverston. Xan's father had been the vicar, years earlier, and Frances attended services there. Mark, utterly atheist, had made no objections; the wedding day was women's business, and a church was as good a venue as any other. The man was nerveless.

Mark and Andy took the tiny front pew, and behind them were Frances, John, Xan and Helen. Helen's hand stole into Xan's; she always got soppy at weddings and he knew exactly what she was thinking. They'd been engaged once, after all. Xan squeezed her hand and stole a glance at her. Oh, she was still beautiful. He leaned over to whisper to her: 'Divorce Andy, marry me. Just for a while? Just so we can have a big white wedding like this.'

'No way. You just want to wear a big flouncy frock,' Helen whispered back, but her hand stole to his thigh. Frances coughed meaningfully. Helen ignored it.

Xan smiled to himself. He knew that he looked gorgeous, for all the good it did him: the only two women he wanted turned his marriage proposals down on a disturbingly regular basis. He whispered again, 'Why do you keep turning me down?'

'Because you keep asking. Now shush, she's here.'

Xan closed his eyes and his ears, letting the next few minutes rush by him. If he ignored the ceremony, maybe it wouldn't matter. He fantasised about someone – himself, John, even Andy – pronouncing that this wedding was a fake, that the groom's real mate was only a few miles away, with his babies. He kept his silence.

The afternoon reception went well, and Xan and John obediently followed instructions and squired Katie's young bridesmaids, teenage cousins of hers. The girls were initially awestruck by the company, but Xan and John were polite and attentive, and did their best to be nothing more than boring older men. Both of them stayed sober. After the meal and the speeches, Xan got a taxi home to get changed and check that Diana was OK. She was gone.

He searched the house and found that she'd tidied up, stripped her bed and washed and ironed her sheets. She'd not left for good; there were still baby clothes and a couple of changes of clothes of her own in a box in the spare room, but she'd clearly not just nipped out to do some shopping. His car was gone too. He found a note, telling him where she'd left it. He got another taxi to Lancaster station, where he picked it up and drove back to the reception.

Mark and Katie were holding court, and he tried to catch Mark's eye. Mark ignored him, so he went to John.

'Aye, she'll probably be feeling down, poor lass. Don't worry, she's probably just gone home.'

'You don't think she's done anything daft, do you?' Xan tried to keep his anxiety out of his voice.

'Diana? She's only ever done one daft thing in her whole life, and that was choosing Mark instead of me. She'll be fine.' John rolled his eyes. 'Our bridesmaid friends have found other entertainment – I think we were too boring. There goes our reputation.'

'Yeah, well, I'm not mad enough to seduce Katie's cousin, that's just asking for shit,' Xan muttered. He had an idea, and searched through the flower arrangements until he found a business card. He ordered flowers for Diana, crazy amounts of them, knowing that it wouldn't be the flowers that would amuse her, but the overabundance of them. He imagined her face as she answered the door and smiled to himself. After half an hour, he tracked down another florist and repeated the order, just for fun.

Night fell, and he went outside for some cooler air and a break from the hard work of socialising with Katie's friends and his own business acquaintances. Mark found him sitting on a wall, staring at the moon.

'Hey,' Mark whispered.

'Hiya gorgeous,' Xan replied, not thinking. 'How's married life?'

Mark laughed; he had the nerve to sound happy. 'Good, so far. Isn't she beautiful?'

'Which member of your harem are we talking about?' Xan bitched.

'That's rich, coming from you,' Mark said, after a shocked silence.

'I just fuck 'em, you won't let them go.'

'And yet you're actively encouraging John and Diana to be together,' Mark said, his voice very calm.

Xan froze. 'It's for the best.'

'As you see it? You don't have the right to make that judgement.' Mark fell silent, and Xan considered his response. Before he could speak again, Mark continued. 'As it goes, I agree with you. I don't have any objections, and I'm glad they're taking it slowly. I just think it would be better for all of us if they wait until I'm back from the honeymoon. I think Diana's upset.'

Xan interrupted. 'D'ya think?' he drawled.

Mark scowled. 'This isn't exactly easy for me. Diana's unsettled and I don't want her to run to John for the wrong reasons. It has to be about them, not about me. I want you to convince them to wait until I'm home. Do you understand?'

Xan stood up. 'I understand you're not happy about John and Diana getting it on while you're on honeymoon, and you've managed to come up with some twisted justification for that. You just won't admit that you like the fact she thinks the sun shines out of your arse, and you don't want John to take that away from you when you're not around to remind her of how fucking wonderful you are.'

'Your mind works in mysterious ways, Alexander Kendrick,' Mark said, eventually.

'Yeah, well, I've been watching you for a long time, Mark Preston, and I know you better than you think.'

Xan walked away, furious.

The party was going well. Xan sought distraction, and found it at the bar, in the shape of a moody barmaid who was getting stroppy about being treated like an idiot. It took only the slightest effort for Xan to get her life story, and for her to confide that she was a postgrad student working for the hospitality company to help get her through her PhD. And yes, she knew who he was, and no, he couldn't have her number, but she'd be happy to take his.

He instantly gave her one of his mobile phone numbers. 'It's answerphone only, but I'll call you back,' he said. 'If you leave your number.'

That amused her, but she took it.

John joined him at the bar, noticing the game and sparing a few minutes to help him reduce the barmaid to a state of hopelessly flattered confusion. He sighed and kissed her hand.

'I'm sorry, I have to go, and I have to steal Xan from you. I hope we meet again.' He bowed. 'Maybe the three of us?'

'Get off,' she said, blushing madly and walking quickly to the far side of the bar.

Xan followed him. 'That's something we've not done for a few years,' he observed. 'D'ya think she'd go for it?'

'Not likely, but it'll fuel her fantasies, and that's fun enough in itself, isn't it? Will I see you later?'

Xan understood what he meant. 'Yeah, sure, I'm almost certain that she's back at her place. Are you leaving? It's only ten thirty.'

John shrugged. 'I'm not enjoying this, and Auntie Fran just asked for a lift home; she said she doesn't want the hotel room, she wants to be at home. I spotted her looking a bit tearful earlier, coming out of the Ladies. She's had enough. Where's your dad got to?'

'He left after the service. Helen and I were hiding in the vestry having a quick snog and he caught us at it. I'm an abomination. Again. Still, whatever. For some reason, Helen isn't – she's my helpless victim. We're never quite sure about Andy, on the abomination-slash-victim scale.' Xan yawned. 'I don't give a fuck, he's a dried-up old prune. My favourite fantasy is that he isn't really my father.'

'No such luck, you've got his receding hairline,' John observed.

'That's right, kill all my hopes and dreams. I'll walk to the car with you – I want to say goodnight to Auntie Fran. Didn't she say that she met Mark's father at a wedding?'

'Nope, my Uncle Anthony worked for her dad, that's how they met, but he proposed at a wedding, on her seventeenth birthday.'

'Nice one Mark's dad! Seventeen? How old was he?'

John shrugged. 'Twenty, twenty-one? Anyway, I think she's missing the old bastard, not that he deserves it, dumping her like he did. I'm going to take her home.'

'To look through her wedding album,' said Xan, feeling romantically sad.

'No photos, there was a fire, she said.'

'Oh, that's tragic.' Xan sighed, then put on a big grin as they approached Frances. 'Hey, Auntie Fran, I hear you're going home with the most eligible bachelor here. Did you catch the bouquet?'

'Behave, child,' Fran replied sharply. 'You're not too big to get your ears boxed.'

'I am, you'd never reach.' Xan laughed, bending just enough to kiss her cheek as he hugged her. She felt fragile, birdlike, in his arms, and he felt a pang of fear for her. 'Are you happy, Auntie Fran?'

'I'm very happy for Mark. It took him long enough to settle down, but I think he did very well for himself. They'll have very clever children, don't you think?'

'Blimey, Auntie, give him a break, he's only just got married!' Xan tried to sound less worried than he felt.

'Yes, but they're not young, are they?' Frances sighed. 'I hope they don't leave it too late, I'd love to see Mark's children.'

As John helped her into the car, he glanced at Xan, exchanging looks of conspiratorial guilt. Frances could never know about her new grandsons.

Xan leaped back as the car roared into life

and sped off. He could have sworn that he saw Frances laugh as he jumped out of the way.

He walked back to the party, thinking about Diana, wondering what she was doing now. He could almost hear the babies, making those funny little noises … those funny big noises, now that he thought about it. He made a mental note to ask Diana if she was sure that John hadn't had some kind of input into fathering them, as the little creatures had amazingly powerful lungs. Back inside, alcohol flowed freely, and now that Mark, Frances and Katie had gone, other substances made an appearance. And, for god's sake, someone had hired a karaoke machine. Helen was on stage, singing. He forgot what a great voice his girl had.

He was watching her when Andy hugged him. 'Xan, you're brooding.'

'Course I am,' he replied.

'I'm fretting about her too. Will you go and check she's OK? Ring me. Let me know. We have to take care of the family.'

'It's a Hearts party, we can't all bugger off,' Xan protested.

'Helen and I will keep things going. I'll tell our parents that you're upset because of your dad. I'll tell everyone else that you had a hot date.'

'I bloody wish I did.' Xan cast one last wistful glance towards the bar and left.

Chapter 27

It was a long drive to Diana's and he was tired when he got there. He let himself in. The house smelled soapy. Everything was unnaturally clean, with not a speck of dust anywhere. The living room curtains and cushion covers were new. She must have been very, very bored.

She was in the kitchen, washing the lampshades. The glass and plastic ones were drying on a thick layer of towels spread on the table. She was gently sponging at the fabric ones from his room and the other spare rooms. She didn't turn round.

'Hey,' he whispered, but got no reaction; she just squared her shoulders.

He wanted to hug her, to put his arms around her and tell her that things would work out, tell her that he didn't care that she was a Shapeshifter, that nobody would, not if she told them in the right way. Then again, his own father considered him an abomination for being voraciously bisexual and glorying in it. He'd never quite worked out whether it was his obvious enjoyment of his sexual exploits, his bisexuality or his tremendous appetite that bothered Mr Kendrick senior. Maybe it was the combination of the three … Still, he thought that if people like his dad could get so worked up about a bit of healthy fun, then there'd be people out there willing to hate Diana, John, Mark and Andy for their abilities. The kids too.

Diana was still ignoring him – not even a 'Hello, Xan' to welcome him back. He went upstairs to find her bedroom door open and the babies in a nest in the middle of the bed. He sat next to them, watching them, suddenly aware of the fact that he stank of spilled beer, smoke and perfume. He reached out to touch the babies and they instantly opened their eyes and started to cry. He tried to comfort them, but they didn't know him, wouldn't accept him. He was panicking when the door opened wider and Diana picked them up, one in each arm. They quieted immediately. John had just arrived, and was behind her, already changing to his wolf form. The magic never grew stale for Xan; it always felt like a privilege to watch the transformation from human form to another. John lay on the floor and Diana put the babies next to him. They clutched at his fur and burrowed closer.

Xan got the message: he wasn't wanted, wasn't needed. John was the substitute father who Diana wanted for these kids. She picked the twins up again and put them back in their little nest. John was changing back, already looking at Diana longingly as he regained his human form. She turned round and John blinked and adopted a straight face. Diana looked at him, and breathed faster.

Xan watched them. They were such a perfect couple; why couldn't they see that? John turned away, muttering something about leaving the mother with her cubs, and Xan cast one backward glance before following John out.

John was breathing heavily by the time he got to the room where he usually slept. 'I love her,' he said.

'Yeah, I know.'

'Mark spoke to me, he said that if she wanted me tonight, it would be because she was angry with him.'

'Mark's a sneaky bastard,' Xan observed.

'Yeah, I know, but I don't want to take that risk. I want it to be about us, not him. I don't mind sharing, it actually feels right.' He laughed. 'Hell, I'm such a fool, she won't be interested in sex yet, will she? Not so soon after the birth.'

Xan had no answer. 'The babies like you,' he said.

'Yeah, they do. They're cute as hell. You and Diana are going to have some sleepless nights with them.' John was looking straight ahead, his expression unreadable.

Xan sighed and took a chair. 'Go to her now. She wants you. Even if she's not ready to fuck, you can at least hold her. That's what she needs.'

'You can do that,' John said. 'I'm … I'm too scared to risk being sent away again. I messed up once, I don't want her to think that I'm making a move now, when she's vulnerable. You go, you go and do … whatever it is that the pair of you do.'

Xan's guts went cold, twisted. He spoke as gently as he could.

'I share her bed, sometimes. We talk. Sometimes we hold each other.'

'Thank you for sparing my feelings,' John

said calmly. 'I'd like to be alone now. I'm still trying to sort out how I feel about Mark making those fake wedding vows, in front of his mother, too. How could he do that?'

Xan had no answer, so he turned and walked back to his own room. He couldn't sleep. He found his book and read for a while, but couldn't concentrate. He listened out for the sound of John's footsteps, or Diana's, on the landing. All was quiet. He couldn't bear it; he had to talk to her, tell her what John suspected. He went to her room. She was awake as soon as he opened the door, aware of him in a different way from before. John was right, she was a mother wolf with cubs now.

'I can't sleep, I'm lonely,' he said.

'Sleep with John, I've already got two babies here,' she said.

'Oh.' He turned and went back to his room, then carried on, to John's room. John sat up as he pushed open the door.

'What now?' John's voice was just on the thin edge of patience.

'You'll never believe this, but she just told me to sleep with you.'

'What?' John rubbed his eyes. 'What?'

Xan smiled. 'No, not like that. She doesn't want me around tonight. Maybe she's hoping that you'll visit?'

John lay back. 'What did she actually say?'

'She said she already had two babies with her,' Xan reported faithfully.

'Ah, Xan. Go to sleep.' John dropped his

head to the pillow and Xan timidly lay beside him.

'In your own bed,' John said.

'Ah, I won't even ask for a cuddle!' Xan whispered. 'Just let me listen to you breathe. It'll help me to sleep.'

John closed his eyes, and Xan took silence for assent. John muttered another complaint, but was soon asleep, and Xan soon followed.

John was already out of bed when Xan woke up. Last night's clothes were still on the floor and a wet towel was flung over the end of the bed. Xan could hear his friend downstairs, singing lustily. He grabbed a quick shower and got dressed. John smiled at him as if nothing could possibly be wrong with the world, and Xan wondered for a moment if the singer had visited Diana sometime during the night.

'How long have you been up?' Xan asked carefully.

'Fifteen minutes. I slept like a log. Want breakfast?'

'Oh yes.' Xan looked hopeful. 'Full works?'

'Our little mother has been shopping. She's got a full fridge and I'm going to empty it.' John's smile was wicked. 'If she wants to argue about it, at least we'll be communicating with each other, yeah?'

Xan heard footsteps on the stairs and felt guilty about talking about Diana behind her back. He threw himself on to the sofa, hiding behind a music magazine. He sensed that she was looking at him and smiled, ready for the joke, the affectionate comment, ready for her to make up for how much she'd slighted him the night before.

'It's upside down, wretch,' she said. Her voice was casual, uncaring. Why should she care? She had her werewolf sons and had John whenever she chose to accept him. Xan was just a nuisance. He lost his temper.

'Why are you being such a bitch to me? This is not my fault. If you'd asked Mark not to marry Katie, he would have listened to you. Now he thinks it's OK to live this weird double life! You had the perfect opportunity and you've blown it. And now you're picking on me! What the hell have I done? You made it quite clear last night that I wasn't part of your precious pack. It's *not* my fault.'

'Grow up or get out,' she said. There was an edge to her voice, and he died a little. That was it, wasn't it? She didn't have time for him now that she had the babies. He'd been congratulating himself on being a grown-up, on providing support for her during her lonely pregnancy, and she'd seen him as … what? A pet? A substitute kid?

'After all I've done for you? And you treat me like an outsider still!' he shouted, incredulous.

'I didn't ask you to do anything for me,' she said.

'You just disappeared! Do you know how that made me feel? I thought I was your friend, that you trusted me. I went home to make sure you were OK, and you'd gone. Didn't you think I'd care? Didn't you realise that I'd worry about you and the babies?'

She looked less sure of herself now. 'Xan, I

couldn't stay in that house. I needed to come home, to my own place.'

'My place *is* your place,' he insisted. 'Just like this is my home too. You don't have to be so tough and independent all the time. That's all I'm saying.' That was enough. He couldn't bear to fight with her. He hid behind the magazine again, trying to calm down before he said something really stupid.

John was whistling loudly in the kitchen in a blokey 'I can't hear any of this' sort of way.

It was unbearable. Xan spoke again, blurted it out. 'And poor John, you have no idea what he's been going though. He's in love with you!'

A plate crashed to the floor. The whistling stopped and the back door opened and slammed shut. Xan and Diana stared at each other.

'Now look what you've done!' she yelled.

'Me? I'm not the one drooling over married men and hiding behind…'

'Hiding behind what? What am I hiding behind?'

'Me, you've been hiding behind me for months.'

'I have not.' Her eyes were wide, her cheeks had a hectic flush.

'Yes you have. You won't stay in the same room as John if I'm not there. You use me. Why do you want me around, anyway?' he sounded bitter, even to his own ears. The babies started to cry upstairs. 'You and your bloody 'pack'. None of you really know anything about 'packs', you're making the whole thing up as you go along! You throw yourself at Mark, sigh over John, and don't think I've not noticed the way you look at Andy when his back is turned!'

She took a deep breath and slammed right back at him. 'You don't want to fuck me, and I don't fuck normals. I thought we were clear on that. And I'm not the one who started this sleeping together business.' The babies were screaming now.

'John thinks we're fucking,' he said quietly.

She stood, stricken. 'Why? What? Have you said something to him?'

'Oh, for god's sake, woman.'

She sat down suddenly in the armchair, sinking into it, horrified. 'Tell me he doesn't.'

'He does,' he insisted. He moved closer, looked at her face. 'Well, is that a tear? Is Miss Superhuman finally showing some bloody emotion?'

'Leave me alone,' she choked

'No.' He shook his head. 'Why aren't you with John? We all know you two are in love, and it's got nothing to do with the pack.'

'Mark…'

'Newsflash, honey: Mark is on honeymoon with Doctor Katie. He's turned his back on you, on your kids, and do you know what he said to me? He as good as said "Keep an eye on my girl for me, I don't trust her with John." He said that at his fucking wedding reception. He's got you on a lead, and if you don't sort yourself out, he'll have you muzzled and chained before the year is out.'

'He wouldn't say that.'

'Think about it, babe … ah, there's the

reaction. Are those real tears?'

'Leave me alone!' She raced upstairs.

He waited, counted to ten and followed her. His blood was up. Oh, but he loved a good fight, once he knew that he was winning. He stepped into her room. 'I'm sorry, I guess I just wanted a reaction from you. It's not normal, the way you've been acting.'

She'd picked up the boys, who looked sleepy and well fed. They'd been disturbed by the raised voices, but Diana's presence soothed them. They calmed her too. Xan took a deep breath, and accepted her hug and her apology.

'I'm sorry too, I've been a bit insensitive, haven't I?'

He looked at her; they were both breathing fast. She felt so soft and pliant in his arms, so utterly female. His hand was at her jaw and her pulse was fast, almost violent in its intensity.

'Put the boys down,' he suggested. She did.

She would speak, she would tell him to leave, she would be sensible. He depended on her to be sensible.

She kissed him.

Oh fuck oh fuck oh fuck. 'We don't do this,' he said.

She kissed him again, and he summoned every defence he had. He was not going to make love to her. He wasn't going to risk their friendship. He wasn't going to do this because he knew exactly how John would feel about it.

She kissed him once more, and he bent her

over, drawing her to him. She was wearing a fitted dress and he reached between her shoulder blades and unzipped it all the way to the base of her spine, slipping his hand inside and caressing her bottom.

He protested, begging her to make him stop, because he couldn't, not any more. She started to tell him how stupid this was, all the time pressing against his cock, her hands in his hair. She told him to make her stop.

One last protest – he couldn't have said who it came from – and they were staring at each other, knowing what was coming. Nothing could have kept them apart.

'Trust me,' he whispered. He didn't know what he meant. He reached into his jeans for a condom, and she demurred. She didn't want it, didn't need it, some complicated werewolf explanation that he didn't care about. She did trust him. They were laughing now, this was good, it wouldn't hurt their friendship. She'd enjoy this, she'd understand that she didn't have to be faithful to Mark, she'd go to John…

He paused. She'd go to John. Could he deal with that? She pulled him closer, kissed him again and opened up to him. Oh, so sweet. He could deal with anything; this was enough to last them a lifetime. She was tight and slick around him, and obviously enjoying it. He relaxed, realising immediately that she was inexperienced and didn't know how to deal with his height or with the fact that, quite simply, he wasn't Mark. She was clumsy, but he would never, ever tell her that. He had to get into a position where he could kiss her, because she was so much shorter than him. Mark wouldn't have any problems. The thought came to him, caught him off balance. This woman was Mark's lover. She was crying out now beneath him, giving herself up to him. He realised that he'd not had this much fun in ages, and let himself go. If this was the end, for once and for all, it was good enough.

He heard a door slam behind him, and then another, downstairs. She was still beneath him, her eyes closed, an expression of utter defeat on her face.

'Was that who I think it was?' he asked.

It was. John had come back to apologise and his suspicions had been confirmed.

He rolled away and lay on the bed, watching the dancing shadows on the ceiling. She kissed him one last time, questioning. He opened his eyes.

'Are *you* mad at me too?' she asked. Her voice was level, but he could see fear in her eyes.

'Oh no, honey, never that. I'll go and look for John.'

She was looking at the babies, for the first time realising how much they tied her down. 'Tell him I'll do whatever he wants,' she said.

'I won't tell him that, not in the mood he's in!' Xan touched her face, and managed a smile. 'It'll be fine. I promise you, it'll be OK.'

He got dressed – there was no time to shower. He needed to find his friend as quickly as possible to make things right.

He left through the back door, the one that

John had used, and made his way down the alley at the side of the house. There was no sign of John's car. His own car was parked perilously close to the house; neither of them had been particularly subtle about parking the night before. He'd try John's flat first, then the lakeside house and the Ransomes' place. He tried to ring him on his car phone. Nothing, no answer.

Trying to find a space to park near John's flat was next to impossible, and after driving round for ten minutes he simply abandoned his car and decided to pay the fine. He used his key. The flat was empty, clean and looked like it hadn't been used for days. Of course, John had arrived at Xan's place a couple of days before the twins were born, and hadn't been home since. Xan walked through, checking it out. When he got to the bedroom he stopped, wide-eyed. There were clothes everywhere, and the bedside drawers had been pulled out and upturned. A strongbox lay open on the bed. Xan leafed through the documents, John's birth certificate, his will, medical card, bank details. No sign of his driving licence or passport. Xan tidied the papers away and returned the box to its usual hiding place, inside the box springs of the bed.

He rang the Ransomes but got no answer. He rang his own number, and played back his messages. He listened to Andy's voice.

'Xan? We've decided to go on holiday. I guess Mark will want to start work on another album when he gets back, so I'm going to make the best of the next month. Join us if you want, I'll call you again when I know where we're going.'

He decided that it was unlikely that John would be at the Lake or the Ransome place, and decided to go straight back to Diana's, being more careful this time about where he left his car.

'I can't find him. I must have missed him by minutes. I think he has his passport with him. He could be anywhere by now. Andy and Helen have gone on holiday, I don't know where…'

He only realised how dull his voice had been when Diana hugged him.

'Hush, sweetie, it'll be OK. Do you want me to see if I can track John down? If I go to his flat later tonight I could perhaps go wolf and get more of an idea of where he went?'

'You could try. I can't see it giving us more of a clue than "he went to his car", but—'

'But I'd know if he was alone or not,' she said, too brightly.

It hadn't occurred to him that John might call up an old girlfriend and take her with him somewhere.

'There hasn't been time for that. He went straight to the flat and left again.'

'OK, then I'd know if he's been back.' She was determined to try this. Xan gave her the key and the address, and just after midnight she left the babies with him and slipped out into the night.

She got back ninety minutes later, looking nauseated.

'What's up? What did you find?' Xan asked.

'I feel ill,' she complained, lying on the sofa

and holding her stomach.

Xan panicked; she was never ill. 'What's up?'

'I changed, just outside the flat. I got his scent, and some more regular ones, probably neighbours. Nobody but him and you have been through the door in the last two weeks. Lots of older scents – he sure has a lot of girlfriends, doesn't he?'

'Did you check inside?' Xan asked.

'Just for a minute. I felt so ill I had to Change back. That's never happened before.' She managed a thin smile. 'Don't worry about it. I think you're right, I think he's gone away somewhere to lick his wounds. We'll hear from him when he's ready. I just wish we could tell him that it didn't mean anything. It was just fun.'

Xan kept his expression neutral. 'Just fun' was one of his favourite expressions, and this was the first time he'd ever realised how bloody hurtful it could be.

'It won't happen again,' he said, not sure if he was asking a question or making a statement.

'No,' Diana said, equally enigmatically. She shook her head. 'No, it won't happen again, I can't see how it could. Next time we quarrel, we'll find a less extreme way of making up, eh?' There was a teasing edge to her voice now.

'Buy me chocolates,' Xan returned, managing to laugh. 'Or send me a card or something.'

They were careful with each other, friendly, even gentle, but she didn't want him in her bed. He went home, and to Andy's, and even rang Frances Preston under the guise of making sure that she was OK. There was no sign of John. He rang the half dozen people that John counted as real friends outside the band and the pack. None of them revealed any knowledge of where he was. Andy got in touch to tell him that they were Ibiza, letting their hair down for a couple of weeks, and Xan was welcome to join them. He was tempted to blurt out the whole story, to get them to come home and comfort him, but he controlled himself and wished them a happy holiday, saying that he wasn't really in a party mood.

He returned to Diana's; there was nowhere else he wanted to be. He'd heard that babies were a trial; noisy monsters that deprived you of sleep and tormented every waking hour. He decided that people were overly sensitive because the twins were funny and cute. Diana was even cuter once she finally succumbed to their charm and stopped referring to them as if they were experimental subjects. They had also finally got the message that he wasn't going to eat them, seemingly recognising him and not screaming as soon as he tried to pick them up. Instead, they screamed when he tried to put them down, which was much less convenient, and meant he had to yell out for Diana to come and help. She laughed at him and soothed them, talking to them in some weird mother language until they quieted. They behaved themselves for her. Nothing stopped her. She was usually carrying one or both of the babies in a sling, feeding them as she worked, and they soon got the hang of things. She expressed surprise when Xan said that she was supposed to sit quietly and let them nurse.

'How the fuck am I supposed to get anything done if I do it like that?' she said, amazed. She did try to relax, though, and the second evening after John's disappearance, Xan found her in the bedroom, listening to Led Zeppelin, dreamily nursing one of the twins.

'Is Stinky not hungry then?' he asked.

'This is Stinky. Poopy's quite happy staring at the ceiling light.'

'Oh. OK. Are we OK, me and you?' he asked.

'We're fine. And you don't have to try so hard to keep your eyes on my face either.'

He smiled. 'I was trying to be tactful.'

'I think we're beyond that,' Diana said.

He sat beside her on the bed. 'Did your mum feed you like this?'

'I don't remember.' Diana smirked. 'Sorry, couldn't resist. No, she didn't.' She was going to say something, but bit her tongue. She took a deep breath. 'I know your mother left when you were a baby. How old were you?'

'Three weeks,' Xan said quietly.

'Oh.' Diana fell silent and he looked away. When he looked back, there were tears running down her face. She wiped at them with her sleeve. 'Sorry, Xan. I don't understand how she could do that.'

'Mark and John's fathers both walked out on

them. They were just little kids then.' Xan's kept his voice steady. 'It's horrible, but it's not quite the same as never knowing your own mother.' He'd opened the floodgates now; the sight of the helpless babies in front of him spurring him on. 'I mean, how could she have known, so soon, that she didn't want me? Was I so bad? People shouldn't have babies unless they know they'll be around to love them.' He reached into the cot and tickled Poopy. 'I'll always be here for the twins. Always.' He gave Diana a challenging glance.

'Good, I'm glad. They'll always need Uncle Xan.' Diana smiled. 'Sleep with us tonight, hey? I promise I won't assault you and I think we both need a cuddle.'

Xan smiled. 'Better not. Give me another few days, let me forget how luscious your arse is. OK?'

She blushed madly and he regretted his levity.

'Sorree,' he mouthed, and she gave him a little smile, forgiving him. She put the older baby back in the cot. Xan reflected that it was about time they came up with better names for the kids, otherwise school was going to be hell for them.

'Xan?'

'Yeah?'

'I won't let you down. I won't leave you. Wherever I am, there'll be a place for you.'

He smiled. 'I feel the same way about you, munchkin.' He took one last look at the pretty tableau and left, feeling safer, somehow.

Chapter 28

A few days later, Andy rang again, puzzled and upset. He'd spotted John the night before, in a bar, with a couple of women. John was almost unrecognisable; with his hair cut short and bleached blond, Helen had walked straight past him! Andy had turned back to speak to him, but John had slipped away. Andy was hurt – he wanted to know what had happened.

'Did Diana piss him off?'

Xan and Diana confessed all, taking the tongue-lashings that Andy unmercifully meted out. When the call was over, they looked at each other like scolded children.

'At least we know where he is now, and that he's OK,' Xan said.

'Yeah, I'll go and find him,' Diana said.

'You'll do what?' Xan shook his head. 'You can't leave the twins. You can't take them with you either, they're too young for that kind of heat. And you certainly can't go wandering around Ibiza with two tiny babies asking if anyone has seen John Preston!'

Diana managed a smile. 'Point taken. We'll ask Andy to find out which hotel he's in, and I'll ring him, or write to him.'

'I'll find him. I'll tell him that you have no interest in me, it was a stupid mistake, and that you want him.'

'Love him,' Diana said, instantly.

'And that you love him: gotcha.'

She was looking at him expectantly, and he nodded. 'I'll go now. I just need to nip back home and get my passport.'

'You look very pretty,' she said, warning him. Yeah, he looked like Xan Kendrick, not like the ubergeek who usually walked out of her front door. For once, he didn't care. If anyone said anything, she could be his cousin, or maybe he could just tell everyone to stuff it. She was his best friend, and he could walk in and out of her house whenever he wanted to.

He stopped at the door and looked back. She seemed about to say something, but changed her mind. She settled for 'be careful', and he walked out, whistling.

He got to Andy and Helen's villa by evening, but there was no sign of John. He conferred with Andy privately, who had told Helen that Xan had whinged so much about Mark's marriage that John had lost his temper and stormed off. She accepted that version of events.

'I reckon he's holing up during the day,' Andy said. 'One of those big anonymous tourist hotels would be about right for him. He blanked me and walked away, twice. Do you think he'll listen to you?'

'I'm his link with Diana,' Xan said. 'Whether he likes it or not. He'll talk to me. I'll start searching tonight. Meanwhile, I'm going to hang around the beaches, see if I can pick up any gossip.'

At the first bar he came to, he took a seat

and leaned forwards.

'This isn't the start of a dirty joke, OK, guys? Now, have any of you seen a bloke, English, about five eight, five nine? Nice muscles, bleached blond hair cropped short, he'll probably have dark roots by now. Straight as fuck but you'd never guess to look at him … Dark brown eyes. Very dark brown eyes. Pretty face, too pretty for his own good… Seen him?'

'No, but I wish I had,' came the predictable response.

'OK. If any of you do see anyone like that, leave a message for me with the bar here. I'll check back every few hours. My name is Alex.'

'Boyfriend?' someone asked.

'I said he was straight,' Xan said, not smiling. 'Brother.'

'Yeah, sure.' Someone laughed as Xan turned and walked away.

He moved on to the next bar. He started asking questions, describing John again. Nobody had seen him. Another bar, and another, until at around two o'clock an overweight redhead with more freckles than skin claimed to have spotted him. She told him the name of the bar where she'd seen John the night before, and gradually let it be known that she'd recognised Xan, and guessed who he was looking for. She didn't know which hotel John would be in, but did know her own room number, and if Xan wanted some no-strings fun with a discreet divorced lady, she'd be back in her room after lunch.

There was something about her hair, maybe something about the way she smiled… Xan grinned and suggested they be sociable and lunch together, and allowed himself to be whisked away to eat paella in a shady courtyard restaurant. The heat, the sunlight and the holiday atmosphere raised more than his spirits, and mid evening he left the woman sleeping, feeling pretty pleased with himself.

He checked in at the first bar, but there was still no sign of John, and he rang Diana to make his report. She reminded him that he was there to look for John, not to get distracted, and he humbly confessed to a distraction, but promised to find John and make things better. She evidently had nothing to say to him and hung up after an awkward pause. He rang her back immediately, teasing her, telling her that nobody hung up on Xan Kendrick and got away with it. She let him hang up that time, and he held on to the phone for a while, wondering how it would work out when she and John were lovers at last. He was beginning to find some hope that they'd make room for him in their family.

It was pretty late when he got a definite tip that John was in one of the more expensive clubs on the island. He pushed his way through the crowd, glad of his height, looking around for his friend. The bar was probably his best bet.

'Xan? Xan Kendrick? What the holy fuck are you doing here?'

He blinked and stopped at the sound of such a familiar voice.

'Jen? Jen, baby?' She was pushing towards

him, followed by some weird-looking guy who was scowling at him. He hugged Jen. 'What are you up to these days? I heard the label had dropped Oaf Uckitt. Are they mad?'

Jen grinned. 'One-hit wonders, that's us. But it was great while it lasted. How the hell are you, Kendrick? Oh, this is Evan. We're going to find somewhere quieter. Do you wanna come?'

'I'd love to, but I'm looking for John.'

Evan broke in. There was something weird about his eyes. Then again, this was a club in Ibiza, there was something weird about the eyes of eighty per cent of the people there.

'I dunno who you think you are, but you can't just go throwing your weight around and going off with people's girlfriends.'

'I quite agree.' Xan was off balance, and surprised at Jen's poor taste in men. 'May I compliment you on your luck, Evan?'

He felt a blow to his stomach and tried to double over, but the crowd was too thick and he felt himself lose contact with the ground and get carried away. Jen was yelling at Evan, then she screamed and tried to get closer to Xan. He did feel awfully light-headed; Evan must have punched him somewhere important. He was on the floor, and some kid was screaming. He closed his eyes, thinking this was all very embarrassing. Someone lifted his head up and he opened his eyes again. He sighed with relief.

'John. I've been looking for you.'

'Shush, save your strength, it's OK. Lie still,

you've been stabbed.'

'Stabbed? Shit.' Xan tried to sit up, to look at the damage, but the calmness in John's eyes made him lie back. 'Hey, at least you can't beat me up now – you'll have to wait until I'm better.'

John leaned closer, but his voice seemed very distant. 'Why would I want to beat you up, hon?'

'Diana…' Xan breathed.

'Oh, that. Forget that. I'm an idiot. It'll all be OK. Is that why you're here?' John's voice seemed to be breaking up.

'Yeah. I'm sorry, we're both sorry.' Xan felt a moment of anxiety, it was getting harder to talk, to make sense. 'She says she loves you.'

'Ah, that's good. She loves you too, you know that?'

Xan smiled. 'She's like my big sister,' he said. 'Or my little sister. Whoops, that's naughty.'

He blacked out, but John brought him back, shouting at him, telling him to hang on for the ambulance. He was saying that Helen was coming.

Xan opened his eyes again and they were there: John, Andy, Helen. Helen was trying not to cry, and he wanted to tell her that it would be OK and that everything always worked out for the best. They were all kneeling on the floor around him. Andy and John were conferring, very quietly, and then John nodded and bent to kiss Xan on the forehead.

'I love you, mate, hang on,' John whispered, then stood up and left, pushing through the crowd.

'Hang on…' Xan whispered, as Andy and Helen kept the crowd away. He was too tired to talk to them; getting stabbed really took it out of you. The lights were on – that was weird – it kinda ruined the atmosphere.

'I'm cold,' he complained, hoping he didn't sound too whiny. Andy lay next to him and held him close, in front of all those people. Dad wouldn't like that, Dad would say he was an abomina…

It stopped hurting.

Epilogue

Anthony was impatient to finish his shift at the docks. He'd heard the words 'Ransomed Hearts' on the radio, which wasn't unusual, but this was in a news bulletin. He finished dead on time and bought a newspaper on the way back to his lodgings.

The story was on page two, and his blood ran cold as he glimpsed the headlines. Murder. Ransomed Hearts. He read on, and was briefly ashamed of his relief when he found out that the victim was the drummer, the Kendrick boy. He read the whole story and found nothing to confirm his dread that the White Pack knew who Mark and John were. There was more news, though: the story mentioned that Mark Preston was not holidaying with the rest of the band in Ibiza, he was honeymooning with his new bride, an English surgeon named Katie.

Anthony binned the newspaper and fought his instincts. Staying away from his family had kept them safe so far; it was better for all of them if he stayed away.

But it was so hard.

Acknowledgements

Thank you

To Mum and Grandma, who made sure there were always books to read.

To Adrian, for everything.

To Hannah Kate, Dea and Fiction Feedback..

To Jon, for a brilliant rock'n'roll cover.

To Dave Harrison who kept telling me that I could do this.

Lightning Source UK Ltd.
Milton Keynes UK
UKHW040436280822
407873UK00003B/431